VALKYRIE CONCEALED

ALLYSON LINDT

This book is a work of fiction.

While reference might be made to actual historical events or existing locations, the names, characters, places and incidents are either the product of the author's imagination or are used fictitiously, and any resemblance to actual persons, living or dead, business establishments, events, or locales is entirely coincidental.

Manufactured in the United States of America
Acelette Press

For my eternal dragon

PROLOGUE

1992 LOS ANGELES

Seeing the one they love die over and over again could jade a god. Especially a god who existed because people worshiped passion and life. Losing the woman he loved five times had made Min wary.

As he watched Kirby sunbathe on an inflatable raft in the pool, a lazy smile on her face, it was easy to believe this was it—she was here to stay. The sun caressed her smooth skin, teasing over pink nipples and the thin strip of blond that covered the *V* between her legs and matched her hair.

It was a little cold for swimming, as far as Min was concerned, but Kirby didn't care for *too hot* after being deployed in the Kuwait desert for several months.

"You could join me, instead of watching from afar," she called from her floating island. She turned her head to the side and dipped down her sunglasses, to meet his gaze. Her eyes were the same crystal blue as the water, and a smile played on her face.

How long had she been here? Safe? Away from war and danger? Did he dare let hope push away trepidation? If he were feeling bold, he'd imagine her being here in a year. In five. As the calendar struck 2000 then flipped into a new millennium.

"The view is incredible from here. Persuade me to leave it behind," he said.

"Hmm... How am I ever going to do that?" Kirby trailed her fingers in the water, twisting her raft until her feet pointed in his direction. She propped one leg up at the knee, offering a perfect, teasing view of her pussy. "I guess I'll enjoy myself out here." She glided her fingers down her stomach.

"You know the rules, Huntress." He let a hint of warning slide into his voice. If she did this now, he'd watch and he'd enjoy the show, but she'd be spanked after, and nothing more.

Which she chose always depended on her mood.

A distant *bang* echoed in the distance, and then another. Fireworks? Backfiring car?

Kirby's hand froze and a frown crossed her face. "Gunfire."

The next few shots were closer. Several blocks away, but near enough to dial up his concern. It was ridiculous to think a random shooting would impact Kirby, but her deaths didn't tend to be predictable.

"Get out of the pool," Min ordered.

Kirby half-sat and stared at him with one raised eyebrow. Her lips were pursed.

His commands were supposed to be for playfulness and sex, but she didn't put up with being told what to do in other circumstances.

He didn't care if this angered her. Only one thing terrified him—her dying. "*Now.*"

Kirby twisted her mouth but quickly climbed from the pool. She tugged on the oversized T-shirt sitting on a chair near the water, and joined him inside.

"I'm all right." The irritation was gone from her voice. "Whatever's going on out there, it's not here." The slight tremor in her words contradicted their reassuring nature. She could block out the memories of her deaths most the time, but not always. There were still nights when the pain and fear woke her up from a deep sleep. Still days when the haunted shadows of her pasts lingered in circles under her eyes.

Min led her farther into the house, toward the home theater he'd set up in the basement. It was safer, tucked away from the outside world, with several walls between the streets and Kirby. Easier to focus on her being here.

He settled onto one of the leather sofas in the room, and pulled her into his lap to straddle his legs. He cupped her face between his hands. "I can't lose you again. There are days when I barely believe you're still here."

"But I am." Kirby's smile was sweet. Innocent. The way she pressed her heat against him was anything but. "If you want a more visceral reminder, I was in the middle of something before we were interrupted." She was naked under the shirt, and her dampness practically burned through his lightweight trousers.

There were also days Min was certain the constant threat of death helped get Kirby off. She'd never struck him as being self-destructive, though, so it didn't matter. She ground against him, and he gripped her hips hard, pinning her in place.

He glided his hands to her ass and squeezed tight enough to earn himself a gasp. "I don't want you to finish things the way you started them. I need to feel you." Desperately and completely.

He shoved her shirt out of the way and lowered his mouth to one breast, while he kneaded the supple flesh. He traced hungry patterns over her skin, tasting sunshine and chlorine and that distinct flavor of *Kirby* that had lived with him for centuries.

She arched her spine as she dug her nails into his back, pressing into his mouth, scratching along his exposed shoulders, and holding him in place.

Like this, he could happily drown in the noises she made and the warmth of her body. He alternated between breasts, lavishing them with attention—licking, then sucking and nibbling—until Kirby was panting and her hips rocked against his.

Min gripped her hair and yanked her head back, exposing her neck and biting hard enough to mark.

She ground against his erection, her dampness seeping through the thin cotton of his pants. The way her breath came in short bursts was familiar. Intoxicating. She was near climax.

He caught her earlobe between his teeth and tugged. "I changed my mind. I do want you to finish what you started." He pressed his lips to the hollow behind her ear. "Make yourself come." He lowered his head to devour her nipples again.

Kirby slipped her hand between her legs. Her knuckles brushed him with each stroke along her pussy, and her grinding grew more frantic. Potent, uncontrolled whimpers tore from her throat. He sucked harder. The sounds she made when she came were heavenly, wrapping him in aural pleasure.

Min needed to be inside her *now*. He nudged her back, to loosen the drawstrings on his bottoms and free his cock. He dragged the head along her dripping slit but didn't have the patience for more play before he thrust inside her.

Her gasp was hoarse. Exquisite.

He returned his hands to her ass, any ability to restrain himself gone. This was a visceral confirmation that she was real. Here, with him. He set a fast pace, digging his fingers in hard. He spread her cheeks and teased a finger against her rear entrance while he slammed inside her.

She was so eager. So incredible.

He spread her juices back, to lubricate his finger, and slipped a single digit in her ass.

Her cry was throaty, and her gaze unfocused. She was lost in pleasure, and he was lost in her.

When Kirby came again, she clenched around his cock, milking him.

He let go of the last hints of restraint, and orgasm washed over him. He spilled inside her. The sharp, tangibly sweet tang of their auras mingling hit his tongue and wrapped around them both. He loved that feeling. That taste of her pleasure melting into his.

The frantic need flowed away, and they slowed to a stop. Kirby rested her cheek against his chest. He moved his hands to rest on the small of her back. They sat there for a while, consumed by each other and tangled in a cloud of contentment.

He softened and slid out of her. She sighed and snuggled closer. This was perfect. Min never wanted to lose it.

"We should get cleaned up." Her voice was sleepy.

He lifted her enough to move her aside, stood, and scooped her into his arms. In the shower, he took his time cleaning every inch of her. This wasn't about sex; it was about caring for Kirby.

When they were done showering, neither of them was in the mood to put many clothes on.

Kirby stole one of Min's shirts, and he donned a pair of boxers, before they returned to their spot in the theater.

"We should see if there's any news about the gunshots we heard." Kirby sounded reluctant but insistent.

It was an odd contradiction. He grabbed the remote and flipped to the most likely local channel to be broadcasting.

There was news, and it was horrifying.

Kirby sat mostly in Min's lap, as the news played on the TV.

Riots had broken out across the city, after a jury acquitted four police officers for the beating of Rodney King. Min had seen countless violent protests in his life—the oppressed rising up to find justice in a world that didn't grant it to them otherwise—but this felt different.

"Gwydion wanted company." A sadness had sunk into Kirby's tone and lingered, the longer they watched the city around them burn on TV. "We could get away for a few days."

It was a good idea. Take her someplace safe, at least until this blew over. "I have the plane on standby," Min said. "Let's go now."

"Do I need to pack?"

He planted her on her feet, then stood. "You should probably put panties on. Maybe trousers."

"Yes, sir. Dressed and ready to go in five."

He allowed relief to trickle through him, as he followed her to the bedroom. This was probably an overreaction, but the trip would be fun and put his mind at ease at the same time.

A short while later, they were in the car, and Daz was driving them to the airport. They needed to drive past some of the most affected parts of the city to reach their destination, but Daz had found a route that allowed them to skirt most of the riots.

Thick smoke from fires a few blocks away clogged the air. Debris and broken glass lined the street.

The driver's window shattered, and a man pressed a gun to Daz's face. "Out of the car now, you rich fucks."

"Okay. It's yours." Min didn't care to argue. The car was a thing. Easily replaced.

"This isn't going to help you any," Kirby said softly. "There are better ways to get things done."

What was she doing?

She reached toward the front seat. "We can help you. Whatever you need. This is only a temporary solution."

"Shut the fuck up, bitch." The carjacker fired.

Kirby gurgled and slumped back in her seat. Blood ran in dark rivers from the hole in her chest, near her throat.

Rage and grief flooded Min, spilling from him in waves. He was vaguely aware of the carjacker screaming before the sound stopped abruptly, but most of his attention was on Kirby.

"Huntress." He pressed his hands to the hole. "You're a Valkyrie now. This can't... Please don't..."

Glassy eyes stared past him, and her head lolled to the side.

Min's fury grew until it clogged his lungs and consumed his thoughts. Not again. This wasn't fair. It wasn't right.

"I'll find you again." He pressed his lips to Kirby's forehead. And in her next life, things would be different. He would do whatever it took to protect her, no matter how extreme. If it meant keeping his distance, pushing her to love someone else—*anything*.

She didn't deserve to have her life ripped away, over and over, because she'd had the nerve in her first life to save the man she loved.

This wasn't Starkad's fault, though. Or even the fault of the trigger-happy carjacker.

Odin had done this. He was gone, but any god arrogant enough to think they had the right to tweak people's lives for their own gain deserved eternal torment and punishment.

Chapter One

Another street. Another morning. Another building with a perfect view for picking off a target at a distance.

The difference today was that Kirby didn't intend to shoot anyone.

Staring through her rifle scope at Gwydion was a precaution. He was there to intercept and warn a potential that she may have been sold out. Kirby and Starkad were three floors up in the building across the street, to make sure no third party interrupted the meeting.

Potentials were people who might or might not become gods, based on a series of prophecies a fate made centuries ago. Most of the existing gods were okay with letting the ascension happen. A handful—those on the board of The Order of Mistletoe—would rather take potentials out before they became a threat.

It wasn't a coincidence that the potentials on their hit lists had been prophesied to eliminate those same gods.

Kirby was enjoying the scenery and the company while she waited. Her sight stayed mostly on Gwydion, a Celtic trickster god who was far more powerful than he let show. Right now, he looked deceptively normal, sitting at a table at the edge of an outdoor café, sipping coffee and scanning the street. His fair hair, tattoo-scarred skin, and easy posture didn't diminish his muscular frame.

"The summit in Ukraine broke down." His casual voice came over her earpiece, as he scrolled through his phone.

Next to her, Starkad let out a long sigh of disappointment. His appearance was seared into her mind without her looking, not that she ever hesitated to stare when she had the chance. He was tall, blond, and covered in ink. A modern-day Viking. Literally. He'd been Kirby's lover in her first life, when she'd forsaken Odin to keep Starkad from dying, earning herself a nasty curse.

Starkad had come out of the deal with a tortured immortality, where Kirby got the opposite. She'd died a dozen times over the centuries, and was always reborn again. At twenty-six, in this, her thirteenth life, she'd already lived far longer than ever before. And she intended to keep it that way.

"And I beheld when he had opened the sixth seal, and, lo, there was a great earthquake," Starkad said.

Kirby would have rolled her eyes at the biblical reference, but Starkad's meaning struck a concerned nerve. Urd—the fate who wrote the original prophecies—predicted the end of the world. Since none of her stanzas were what they seemed on the surface, it was believed she meant more of a rebirth than a literal end.

That didn't make it any easier for Kirby to hear about the events heralding the world's pending demise. Which was ironic—were her feelings on the matter irony? She was pretty sure they were, since she and Starkad had been working with an entire organization for the last few years, to ensure the prophecies happened.

The alternative was still mass destruction, but on a far more chaotic scale. Mostly because the TOM board members were going to dangerous and deadly lengths to stay alive.

One of them, Hel, had been defeated at Kirby's hand. But not before Hel put a series of orders in place to execute hundreds of people upon her death. She'd told her most devoted—fanatical—followers that it was the only way to bring her back.

Kirby would save Hel's targets regardless; she hated seeing people suffer at the gods' hands. Keeping Hel in her grave was a bonus.

"Where is she?" Kirby grumbled. The target they were pursuing was one she'd saved before. Last time, the woman had a schedule to set a clock by.

Gwydion glanced up. He couldn't see her—that was the point of picking this location to watch from—but she swore he met her gaze through the scope. "Maybe something spooked her and she already ran."

Or TOM got to her first. Kirby preferred Gwydion's assumption. According to Min, this potential was different. Most potentials were terrified to learn they were being hunted. A few seemed to take it in stride. But Azzie had expected the news.

If Kirby followed that logic too far, it pointed at Azzie's walking the same path every day for months because she wanted to be a target. Kirby couldn't fathom putting herself in that kind of danger intentionally.

Other kinds of danger, sure. But Brit had been the person hunting Azzie, and Kirby never wanted to be on the receiving end of Brit's gun again. She didn't want to let that train of thought run. It was hard enough, knowing Brit was still alive, without diving into the seconds—virtual days?—that led up to Brit's not-death.

"How long do we wait?" Kirby asked.

She didn't have to pull her attention from the scope to know Starkad strode to the other side of the room. Since the fight with Hel, she'd felt his presence more distinctly. It was hard to define, but she sensed when either he or Gwydion were near, and she had a vague feeling of their moods without seeing or talking to them.

"You got anything?" Starkad's voice echoed, once from behind her and once in her earpiece. He must be on the phone with someone else.

Azzie's odd behavior was the reason Kirby was here. Other, more direct extraction teams had been sent to retrieve and relocate most of the potentials, but anytime someone found Azzie, she dropped off the radar again.

ALLYSON LINDT

The Followers of Urd had decided to keep their distance once she was located this time. Send in people who were adept at sticking to the shadows and blending into crowds. With Kirby's training as an assassin and Gwydion's power to make most people forget he was in any given location, this team became the logical choice.

"Keep me posted," Starkad said. He joined Kirby again. "We wait until we have more information." The echo was more obvious with him closer.

"A guy can only drink so much coffee in a single sitting." Gwydion's tone was light.

Kirby liked having them both here. "So maybe switch to lager in a couple of hours."

"Real problem solver, you are," Gwydion said.

She'd been concerned about Gwydion's joining them—he was only unobtrusive to people who weren't looking for things that were out of place. That meant he stood out to any TOM operative. However, since they were looking for a woman who'd led a normal, suburban life, not someone trained from childhood to hunt gods, he shouldn't register as important on Azzie's radar.

Having both Starkad and Gwydion nearby kept Kirby's thoughts from drifting into places they shouldn't on a stakeout. Mostly. If she followed the tangents long enough, she always landed back on the last time she and Starkad were protecting this potential—when Kirby realized her ex-girlfriend was the person feeding Starkad information, and Brit was suddenly an unshakable part of Kirby's life again.

Even after Kirby thought she was dead, Brit came back. Min had told Gwydion, who in turn told Kirby, in the most literal game of telephone ever.

And Kirby had agreed to see her again at some point. To not kill her on sight. Why did Kirby keep letting her live, after the betrayals?

The most recent one was to save me.

Or Kirby was suffering from patterns of abuse.

"You're distracted." Starkad was sympathetic. He felt her mood shifts now too.

Though she suspected this one was obvious. "I'm alert enough."

"You're thinking about her. You don't have to see her again."

"For someone who insists they don't care who or what she is, you spend an awful lot of time keeping her out of my life."

"Shooter." One of Starkad's nicknames for Kirby when they were on mission. His use of it was a warning for her to be aware of her surroundings. It was also his way of changing the subject.

Kirby's attention never left the street, and neither would Starkad's. "You brought it up. Now we finish the conversation," she said.

"There's more to say?"

"I want you to admit it." Kirby's own words surprised her.

"Admit what, exactly?"

"You know what."

"What about you and Min?" Starkad countered.

Interesting left turn. "I own the way I feel about him." That was what she wanted to know—how did Starkad really see Brit? "He's an obsessive fuck who refuses to see my point of view." Except he'd gotten it at least a little, when he realized his guy betrayed him to see Kirby destroyed.

Starkad adjusted his position. "I'm an obsessive fuck. You're—"

"Yes?"

"Obsession comes with the territory."

Gwydion snorted in her ear. He must be loving this exchange. One of his favorite hobbies was making Starkad squirm. Though she'd discovered over the past few months the roles were reversed behind closed doors, when clothes started coming off. Gwydion was the reason Starkad had proposed bondage and pain, as a way to help Kirby with her PTSD. In the not-so-distant past, Starkad had done the same for Gwydion.

"Yes, I've got my obsessions too." Kirby recognized that. "But he doesn't understand mine, and I don't get his. I've never made a secret of that. How do you really feel about Brit?"

Another sigh, this one heavy and defeated. "The only reason she's still alive is because of you. I would have had her taken out years ago, for what she did to you, but you were the one who was wronged, and I wasn't going to take the choice of her fate from you. That doesn't mean I want her anywhere near you."

Any retort Kirby had died in her throat. She was finally hearing the full truth.

"Shooter." Starkad's tone was serious now, and a different kind of tension radiated from him.

She gave her scope her full attention. Sure enough, a familiar redhead was strolling toward where Gwydion sat.

A smile on his face, he rose to meet her halfway.

Two men materialized from the shadows, and Azzie had Gwydion pushed back against a wall, knife to his throat.

It all happened so quickly, Kirby's mind raced to process.

Pull the trigger.

She wasn't supposed to shoot a potential, and Azzie probably couldn't hurt Gwydion. But the prophecies had her destroying a trickster god, and they might not be talking about Loki after all.

"The young lady would like you to put down the gun and join us on the street." Gwydion's voice came clearly and calmly over the earpiece.

Why didn't Kirby hear *the young lady* make the request?

She felt Starkad move. He'd be racing downstairs for ground support.

She steeled her voice. "Tell the young lady I have a bead on her and I'll cover you with her brains if she doesn't back the fuck up."

"Don't do that," Gwydion said. "I hate cleaning brains out of clothes." He repeated Kirby's message.

Azzie held her hand over her shoulder, knuckles in Kirby's direction and middle finger extended.

Well, that was a fuck up. Kirby knew better than to make a threat she wasn't prepared to act on.

A hiss in her ear told her Starkad was close. Which meant she had another option

She didn't like this path, but it was their best choice. She'd gotten used to the fact that she couldn't do it without feeling the pain herself. She didn't like hurting others this way, though. Torture wasn't her thing.

It was all psychological, and she'd take the pain away as soon as she was next to Azzie.

Kirby focused on her past lives and the death that accompanied each one. She summoned memories of the pain and shared that pain.

Azzie's dagger clattered to the ground. She screamed, her agony screeching through the earpiece and up into the window, where Kirby sat.

No one in the nearby café so much as blinked. Gwydion was good.

Starkad got the drop on one of the men and pinned him to the ground.

The other man dug his elbow into Gwydion's throat. "Make it stop."

Gwydion raised his hands in surrender. "Holy shit. Finn?"

"Davyn?" Starkad's mutter added to Kirby's discomfort.

She hadn't heard that name in centuries. Not since her first life.

"Stand down," Starkad said.

CHAPTER TWO

The fifteen seconds it took Kirby to pack her gear felt like an eternity. She wanted to blame Min for this, as she raced to the street. Not because it was actually his fault, but because he was in charge of relocating potentials, and that made him a convenient target for any potential-gone-wrong situation.

She was on speaking terms with him, at a professional level. He hadn't pushed the *We promised to love each other for eternity* angle since she sent him away. When he'd told Starkad this girl expected to be relocated, Kirby asked how.

Min's response? *I don't know. I didn't push for more information.* He didn't pry into potentials' lives, as long as they were out of danger.

Look how well that worked out.

Kirby sprinted past Starkad, Davyn's eyes growing wide when he saw her. She pulled up short when the stranger stepped between her and Azzie.

"She can make it stop, Finn," Gwydion said.

Great. Everyone knew someone.

Kirby knelt in front of Azzie and extended her hand, but she didn't make contact. She hated bartering with relief from pain, but she was dealing with a potential god killer, and her men's safety was a higher priority than Azzie's. "Promise me you'll hear us out when I take the pain away," she said.

Azzie gave a slight nod.

Kirby brushed her fingers over Azzie's forehead and visualized drawing out the pain.

Azzie gasped and dropped her head. She shot out her hand and grabbed Kirby's wrist, digging her fingers into the tendon.

So much for hearing each other out.

"You pulled a knife on one of my men." The words were supposed to sound businesslike, but Kirby couldn't hide her possessiveness.

"He's a god. Gods are trying to kill me." Azzie met her gaze.

This was a lot more work than picking an assassin off a potential and moving on. None of the others Kirby saved in the past few months were this much effort. It was refreshing to finally run into a potential who was taking some initiative.

"Min sent us," Kirby said.

"Nice guy, but a lot of people have tried to kill me since he found me."

Kirby hid a wince. They should take this conversation some place less public. Gwydion could keep them masked for a while, but she didn't like being so exposed. "Yeah... He feels real bad about that. But regret doesn't solve problems."

Azzie raised her brows. She was probably Kirby's physical age. In some ways, she looked it.

But her expressions, the way she held herself, and the hint of an easy smile that lurked behind her expression, made her appear a lot younger.

Then again, Kirby had a dozen other lives behind her, adding to her age. "You promised to listen to me."

"Can you teach me that take-away-the-pain trick?" Azzie let go of her wrist.

Kirby grasped her hand and pulled her to her feet. Kirby would have asked about the inflicting-the-dozen-lifetimes-of-pain trick. "Probably not. It's kind of instinct. I touch you, I think about making the hurting stop, and it happens."

"Neat." Azzie looked at Gwydion. "Is the coffee here any good?"

The men had all stood down, though the one who'd turned on Gwydion didn't look happy about the truce.

Gwydion shrugged. "I'd rather have a stiff drink at this point."

"It's nine in the morning," Starkad said.

Gwydion stared blankly at him. "And your point is…?"

"Probably the only time you'll ever hear me say this—I'm with him." The thin man with the pale hair—Finn—nodded at Gwydion. He spoke with a heavy Irish accent.

"You're alive. And you look like you," Davyn said.

Kirby turned to face the berserker. He was at least twelve centimeters taller than Starkad, with a bear-like build. His berserker form was that of a bear. He'd been an ally in her first life. But a lot could change, especially with the centuries that had passed since.

"Same to you. Are we...? Are you...?" She didn't know the best way to ask, *Do you serve a god who wants one of us dead?* He'd always been fiercely loyal. "Who are you fighting for these days?"

Davyn nodded at Azzie. "Don't hurt her again, and you and I won't have a problem."

He worshiped a twenty-five-year-old redhead? He must fit in great in this world.

"We need something other than alcohol or caffeine." Kirby didn't drink, and the last thing this group needed was to be *more* on edge.

Azzie gasped. "We should have donuts."

Hard to argue with that. Sugar didn't solve problems any more than regret did, but it tasted better, and it softened the blow of a lot of things.

Kirby gestured toward a donut place a few blocks away. "I'm in."

Finn stayed by Azzie's side as they walked, and insisted he wanted Gwydion in front of them.

That must be an interesting story. On the surface Gwydion was the least threatening of their group. Sure, he could summon the trees to fight on his behalf, but someone would have to know him, to know that.

Davyn fell back, watching. Kirby and Starkad joined him. His gaze was fixed on Azzie. The only time he took his eyes off her was to do a quick survey of their surroundings. "Thought searching for her would have driven you mad a long time ago," he said.

"It almost did," Starkad said.

23

Kirby had heard so many stories of his past. They'd shared a lot over the last six months. "I didn't think there were any other berserkers left." They were tough, but unless they were like Starkad—cursed by a god or something similar—they weren't immortal.

"There are a handful of us. It's…" Davyn sighed. "Long story. And not nearly as heartwarming as lovers who spent centuries searching for each other. The tail end of my immortality is a blood oath to her mother." He nodded at Azzie. "A promise to watch over her."

That could explain why he was so protective. A blood oath was an unbreakable bond. Going against one meant violent pain and torture, ending with death. But there was more in Davyn's gaze than just a guardian watching over a ward.

"I'm glad you're still around," Starkad said.

Davyn smiled. "Same for both of you. Not around *us*—we'd like to leave you soon. But it's good to see the two of you together."

"Agreed. To all of the above." Kirby tangled her fingers with Starkad's and leaned against his arm. A group like this, full of people various gods wanted dead, was a bad thing to keep together for any length of time. Kirby would stay with Azzie to establish if she was better off on her own or under Urd's protection. Though, she seemed to be doing just fine right now.

At the donut place, Kirby ordered them a dozen assorted, and they pushed a couple tables together in the back corner of the dining room. They made an interesting sight. Davyn and Starkad next to each other, the beasts inside almost peeking through—wolf dining with bear. Azzie sat between Davyn and Finn, looking like she had two scary guardian angels. Or demons.

Kirby suspected Azzie wasn't as helpless as the picture painted. Finn was casting dagger-like glares at Gwydion, so Kirby sat between the two men.

"No one's noticed us since we approached you outside." Finn turned back to Gwydion. "I assume that's your doing. Glad you can do something useful."

What a charming asshole. "I take it the two of you know each other?" She gave Gwydion her attention. She preferred his company over most on any given day, and today that was multiplied. In past lives, he had a similar accent to the new guy, but he could adopt most English-speaking accents without issue these days.

"Fionn McCool is a hunter," Gwydion said.

Kirby swallowed a snort at the name. She understood it didn't have anything to do with how it sounded in a modern tongue, but she couldn't help her amusement.

"It's Finn." He switched his hard glare to her. "And what are you supposed to be?"

"A Valkyrie," she said.

"Sure." Disbelief dripped from Finn's reply. "There are no more living Valkyrie. They all died."

Kirby had no idea if this guy was familiar with the prophecies of Urd—those that said Azzie would become a god, or those that talked about Kirby—but reincarnation was rare and impressive regardless, and she wanted to see him flinch. "So did I. Many times."

"Oh. You're her." Finn's antipathy vanished.

Azzie broke a piece off a donut. "He's a big believer in the prophecies." She popped the cake in her mouth.

"And you're obviously familiar with them." Now that the introductions were out of the way, Kirby could get down to why she was really here. Perfect segue.

"My mother was…" Azzie sighed. "I don't know what you'd call her. She had visions. She raised me on them. They filled in a lot of blanks between the quintets Urd wrote about me."

That explained why she hadn't been surprised to see Min. It also showed how much of a believer she truly was. Kirby didn't know if the prophecies were of the going-to-happen-regardless variety or were the self-fulfilling sort. Most of them were difficult to interpret, and only some had come true.

Azzie crossed one arm over her body and dropped her hand to her hip. A sheathed axe appeared, handle against her palm. "I've been training to defend myself most of my life."

"An axe?" They hadn't taught her to fight with an effective weapon? Kirby looked at Davyn. "Was that your idea?"

"Not everyone can incapacitate people with their minds." Finn sneered.

"No. But most people can hit center mass at close range with a good handgun." Kirby knew how to use an axe. She'd learned in her first life, and honed her hand-to-hand combat skills in this one. But if she didn't have to take the risk, she wasn't going to.

"You sound like—"

Finn settled a hand on Azzie's arm, silencing her. "How beautifully impersonal," he said to Kirby.

"Death is always personal. Anyone who's taken a life either knows that or has taken too many." Kirby didn't like this guy. And if they believed Azzie was supposed to take on Loki, why hadn't they given her more practical training?

"We need to move you some place safer." Gwydion was ignoring the donuts and pretending to ignore Finn. The irritation bristling under his skin was almost tangible. At least to her.

His statement was a giveaway too. They didn't *need* to relocate Azzie. If she was safer on her own, they could leave her be. They were here to warn and assess.

"Because someone sold her out?" Davyn asked.

Finn nodded. "Loki knew where she was, less than a day after FU relocated her. Hel never lost track of her."

Kirby wasn't interested in this becoming a dick-measuring contest. Gwydion and Starkad did that once, at Gwydion's insistence. Starkad won, but Gwydion had the girth over length. The atmosphere here wasn't charged with the same kind of humor.

"Hel is dead now. We have a god killer too." Gwydion hooked a thumb in Kirby's direction.

Hel was dead *for now* would be a more accurate statement. After reviewing Brit's warning, so many months ago, Kirby, Starkad, and Gwydion realized they needed to wait before going into the TOM academy.

Supposedly, interrupting the ritual would make things worse. Hel hadn't laid out an intricate plan that could be disrupted with one missed step. She'd made her resurrection inevitable.

Kirby and her men were working to figure out where the loophole was, and hoping they discovered the answer before it was too late. Too bad they didn't know when *too late* was.

"Hel isn't the god pursuing Azzie." Finn's irritation yanked Kirby back into the conversation. "And full offense—you people have done a shitty job with your protection racket."

Kirby couldn't argue that. She'd grown lax with her trust, giving it to Gwydion and Min because Starkad did, and because her heart and body wanted more from them.

She was lucky things worked out with Gwydion. Min hadn't been the one to sell out the potentials, but someone *he* trusted was. And Min was on his way to making the same mistake with Brit.

"No one's going to stop you from fading into the woodwork." Kirby told Azzie. "If you do, we won't pursue you again. Urd will write you off and leave you on your own."

Azzie grabbed one of Davyn's donuts—her third—and bit into it. She held Kirby's gaze the entire time and washed the food down with a long drag of milk.

Hardly threatening.

"If you were me, would that bother you?" Azzie asked.

Kirby hadn't meant her words as a threat. They were a statement of reality. Not being on Urd's radar would be a relief. The only reason she continued to operate within the system was for access to Urd's resources.

"No. It wouldn't bother me at all," she said. "In fact, if I were you, I'd run as far and as fast as possible from any group of gods and servants larger than the one you travel in. Leave town. Hide. Pretend you never heard of the prophecies."

Kirby wished she could.

CHAPTER THREE

Min was learning to see the world through a different lens. One that showed not just beauty, but also danger. It wasn't a natural instinct. However, since discovering one of his closest associates had been selling him out for years, this new type of observation had become necessary.

Brit parked his car on the street, in front of a cozy ranch-style house with immaculate landscaping. What did she see when she looked at the place? What would Kirby see? Was the car in the driveway normal? Were the neighbors peering through curtains, watching everything?

The man who lived here was a potential god Min had relocated, to keep him off TOM's radar. Was he safe? He was Min's top priority.

Min was reaching out to the lower-risk potentials, offering an apology and another relocation. So far, every meeting had gone smoothly. He wouldn't let himself become complacent, though.

He and Brit stepped from the car and she handed him the keys. One of the many rules—

Starkad's, not Min's—in place, to keep an eye on her. She drove. Surrendered the keys at stops. Only owned items he purchased for her. Agreed to random checks of her luggage and any other belongings.

When Brit had awoken from death, Min hadn't let her go. He'd helped dozens of people relocate over the past few years, and all of them had asked some version of, *am I a prisoner?*

He always told them *no*. With Brit, he didn't hesitate to say *yes.*

She didn't argue or try to run. She agreed to the rules—they were better than life at TOM. And she'd agreed to help with these relocations.

Min only took her help in situations where he could recover if she betrayed him. There had been no sign that was her intention, but Kirby loved to point out lulling the victim into a false sense of security was part of TOM's training.

Brit knocked on the front door and stepped back next to him. She was mostly here to act as firepower, but her presence and appearance—the cute, girl-next-door blonde—greatly diminished the odds of the neighbors calling the cops on a large black man walking around the neighborhood in the middle of the day.

The door opened, and Kyle grinned when he saw Min. "Hey. I wasn't expecting you."

"I'm sorry to drop by unannounced." Min would rather call every one of them, but he wanted to give TOM as few chances as possible to track their movements. He didn't tell Brit where they were going until she needed directions, and never whom they were seeing. She wasn't privy to where potentials were relocated to. No one was, except for Min.

Kyle shook his head. "I was actually just stepping out. I'm in a bit of a rush."

"You need to make time for this." Brit's tone was cool.

Kyle stared at her. "Beg pardon?

The first few meetings, Min had been more polite. Several of the potentials were happy to see him, since he'd given them a large sum of money and offered them a new life the last time they'd talked. But that didn't mean they were looking forward to being uprooted a second time.

Brit sighed. "You have five minutes, and we can't give you privacy. Collect anything sentimental. Leave everything else behind. You'll be provided for in your new location."

Min let her be the enforcer. It came naturally to her. He was operating under the assumption she was near-impossible to kill, based on the fact that Hel tried. He hadn't been as hesitant to test her immortal boundaries as he had been with Kirby. Brit never argued. Min inflicted wounds of progressive severity, to see if she would heal.

She always did, but it wasn't instantaneous, like Min's ability. And injury caused her pain. If she betrayed him, he could disable her long enough to stop her.

"No. I don't have time for this." Kyle's cheer vanished. He started to close the door.

Brit shoved her foot in the opening. "This isn't a negotiation." She wasn't allowed to be rough or get physical—they were here to protect these people. She tended to be imposing, but this level of aggression was out of character for her.

"Please." Min hid his concern about the shift in Brit's behavior. This was a bad time for her to tip her hand if she was going to betray him. But the results would be the most effective for her that way. "Your location may have been compromised, and I want to get you someplace safe."

"Again? No thanks. I'll take my chances."

In the end, it was always the potential's choice, and Kyle had been warned of the danger and consequences. Min rested a hand on Brit's arm, to warn her, pull her back, and disable her if needed. *Disable.* He didn't want to do that.

Brit wedged her foot further in the door, and Min tightened his grip on her forearm.

*

The edges of Min's power licked along Brit's skin, and she clenched her jaw. Kyle wasn't alone in the house. She'd felt *something* in the air as they strode up the walk. A new sensation that screamed *danger*, and she didn't like it.

She stepped back from the door. "My apologies." Her voice was sugar sweet.

Barging in at this point was dangerous anyway. She was off her game if it took the threat of harm to remind her of that. Then again, nothing in her head had been the same since Hel killed her. Brit's training was still there, but parts of it were no longer instinct. In some ways, she felt like a first-year student all over again.

"What was that?" Min growled as they walked back to the car.

33

This situation was a great example. She could see all the variables but didn't know what to do with them. It was causing her to stall. "Keep walking. He's not alone in there. And if it's TOM with him"— which was the assumption—"they know who I am."

"*Fuck.*" Min didn't falter. For a big bossy guy, he took instructions well when needed.

Brit's first impulse was back—the desire to barge in, shoot the threat in the head, and hope no one got caught in the crossfire. *Wrong answer.*

She had to think past that, to an appropriate next step. "He's still alive for a reason. They had him answer the door and tell you *no* for a reason. You drive." She slid into the passenger seat. "Two blocks north, and stop at the convenience store," she said when he was seated.

"Why would they do any of that?" Min's scowl was fierce.

Brit didn't fear much these days. Especially not the teddy bear of a god of sex and life, who adored Kirby more than he did almost anything else. "I'm sure there are a lot of reasons. Guessing won't do us any good. Getting him out alive will."

"Why the convenience store?"

"I want a hat to commemorate our trip. I also want you to ask to use the restroom, take off your undershirt, and loan it to me." She needed a disguise. A baseball cap would hide her hair, and Min's shirt would hide her frame.

A TOM team consisted of two people—a sniper and a spotter. The pair couldn't watch the entire house at once. Brit needed a little luck to figure out which spot they were least likely to be keeping an eye on.

The front door. Brit had approached from that direction once, and no one launched a direct frontal assault.

While Min took care of things inside the convenience store, Brit sketched out next steps in her mind. He returned and handed her the disguise.

"Great." She reached for the door handle. "Leave here, do a wide circle around the block, and return to the house in five. Tell Kyle you're sorry I was so pushy."

Min grabbed her wrist, his grip tight. "You're not going anywhere."

"Where am I going to go? I'll meet you at the house. We'll get your guy out, and then you can lock me away again." She didn't have any magic powers, beyond healing from some pretty serious wounds. She couldn't fly or teleport or shoot lightning. She could hit a target dead center at one hundred meters without a scope. That was the only thing that made her valuable to Min, and the only reason he didn't just lock her up in a cell somewhere, to keep her away from the woman he loved.

When Min showed up alone, they'd start looking for Brit someplace else, but that meant leaving one person with the potential and only one set of eyes for every other angle.

Min let her go. "Don't make me regret this."

She gave him a tight-lipped smile. Sure, if she were trying to win his trust so she could betray him, this was exactly what she'd do, how she'd act, to convince him she meant no harm. But she just

35

wanted him to trust her. Period. *I brought this on myself.* Not as comforting a thought as the first thousand times she'd repeated it, but something she needed to remember.

The walk back to Kyle's house was full of her trying to keep a low profile, while not looking suspicious to anyone who did see her. Much harder to do during the day in suburbia than in the middle of the city.

But the sun was warm on her face, and she hadn't been allowed to wander alone outside since she came back to life. Her spirits lifted as she strolled.

Brit cut a random path between houses before she drew within visual range of any windows in Kyle's place, ducking behind bushes, fences, and cars.

Min pulled up right on time. She couldn't let him see her; he was painfully honest and might tip her hand.

She was close enough to hear him knock again, and to hear Kyle say, "I already told you—"

"I'm sorry about my companion," Min said. "She's a bit hotheaded, and I left her to cool off. It's *imperative* that you hear me out."

A version of the truth. By now, the TOMs would be on alert. Best to get in before they had time to reach more of a conclusion than *she's around here somewhere.* She strode at double speed toward the door, drawing her pistol.

Kyle's eyes grew wide when he saw her.

Brit didn't—couldn't afford to—hesitate. She kicked the door open, caught TOM One off guard, and shot him in the forehead.

"Get down." She shoved Kyle behind her, as a bullet bit into her right shoulder. Pain rocketed through her, and her gun arm went limp.

CHAPTER FOUR

Min watched in horror, as a woman stepped into view across the room, weapon drawn. He yanked Kyle back further, as Brit was shot.

She grunted and faltered. The half second it took her to switch her gun to the other hand didn't give Min enough time to think about next steps. Her body jerked, as another bullet caught her in the chest.

Brit pointed and fired.

The other woman dropped to the floor like a heavy sack.

Brit spun, wobbling on her feet. "Anyone else in the house?"

"No." Kyle looked and sounded terrified.

Min didn't blame him; Brit was bleeding freely.

Min shrugged out of his suit coat, folded it into a tight square, and pressed it to the hole in her chest.

"Thanks." Pain spilled from her reply. "We're leaving now. I'm in no condition to check the rest of the house."

"What about my—"

"*Now.*" Min cut Kyle off, ushering him toward the car.

Brit collapsed in the back seat. Thank creation the upholstery was black leather. It would shrug off most of the bleeding and hide the stains.

Not that Min cared. The car could be replaced. Brit hadn't hesitated to put herself in the line of fire. He'd call it a death wish, if she could die. It hurt, though. She'd willingly taken the hit and the pain, to save a potential.

Starkad was wrong; Brit was redeemable.

"Don't we need to get her to a hospital?" Kyle kept glancing back at Brit as they drove.

"Nah. I'm good." The strain was fading from her voice.

Min sent a message to the cleanup team, letting them know there were two bodies. He kept an eye on traffic behind them. One trick Brit taught him early on—how to spot if he was being followed.

The next steps were simple, compared to what Min and Brit had just been through. When He was certain they were safe, he'd leave Brit in a motel room. A friend had created a portable prison. Min could install it in the room, and Brit could wander freely inside the confines but not leave.

Then Min would get Kyle to a new location, and he'd retrieve Brit when he was done.

"Thank you." Kyle's gratitude rushed out in a heavy breath. "I have to admit I always doubted this whole I-might-be-a-god-thing was real. Those two showed up and told me you were on your way. Said if I made you go away, they wouldn't kill me."

Brit lay back on the seats. "Why didn't you incinerate the assholes?"

"I don't think that way," Min said.

"You need to start."

"No." He made concessions to ensure these potential gods were safe; his information led to deaths, and he was aware of it. "I won't become a cold-blooded killer."

Brit clucked. "Because the thought is revolting?"

"It's certainly distasteful." He was a god of life. Taking it was counterintuitive to his very existence.

Brit sat up. "And you wonder why Kirby doesn't want you around."

Min and Kirby didn't see eye to eye on matters that were critically important to her. Though he saw a little more of her perspective every day, he doubted she saw his. "The act is distasteful, not necessarily the people who have to commit it."

"Fine line. Especially when you insist you're avoiding that very thing, to preserve who you are."

Min saw her point. His phone chimed with a new text, and Starkad's name flashed on the display screen in the center of the dashboard. He glanced at Brit in the rear-view mirror. "It's in my coat pocket."

"Of course it is." She made a series of disgusted grunts, as she fished his phone out. "It says *it's time*."

"Right." The brief phrase carried an enormous weight. The message meant Aeval had found her people—those TOM took before the fight with Hel—and it was time to save them.

40

There were upsides to the message. Seeing Kirby again. Depositing Brit in Aeval's realm, rather than locking her in a room.

It also meant Brit would see Kirby again. And that today's mini-shootout would be the least stressful mission they conducted this week.

****

Kirby always enjoyed visiting Aeval, and despite the reason for it now, today was no different.

The queen of the fae lived in an honest-to-gods castle. Stone walls, turrets, and a sweeping landscape. Inside was a complete contradiction. There was still a throne room and a ball room. A dining hall. Vast bedrooms with four-poster beds.

That was in one wing.

Another was a section for recreation, which included fighting mats, weights, and weapons. And Kirby, Starkad, and Gwydion were waiting in the business wing, in a conference room, complete with leather chairs, a glass table, and a projector at the front.

The entire castle was *high fantasy meets the modern world*, and Kirby loved it. What she didn't love was the nagging reminder that Min and Brit would be joining them. She wasn't ready to see them again.

Additional skilled backup was needed, though. This mission was an extraction, and Brit excelled in those. As long as playing along here suited her purposes, she'd be a solid ally.

Brit wasn't here yet, and Kirby wanted to think about anything else. She wasn't the only one on edge. Starkad stood next to her, back to the wall and arms crossed. Gwydion leaned against the conference table, facing both of them, with the door behind him.

If Kirby wanted a distraction, he'd happily offer one. She adopted a mischievous smile. "So, mister grumpy-god earlier? Sexy-as-fuck accent? How come you never talk like that anymore?"

"Not a clue what you're talking about, lass." Gwydion slipped into an Irish brogue. He grasped her fingers and tugged her closer, then tilted his head next to hers. "Do you want me to whisper tales of leprechauns and banshees and sprites in your ear?" His breath was hot and tantalizing against her skin.

Starkad's sigh made her roll her eyes, but she didn't stop smiling.

"Are you really going to let her do that?" Starkad asked, his tone light.

Busted. Not that Kirby would admit her intent so easily. "Do what?"

"Fuck him, so you can ignore what's coming." Starkad's accurate accusation hit her back.

Gwydion kissed along her fingertips. "As long as *we're* all coming, I'm not too picky about the circumstances."

Kirby reluctantly reclaimed her hand, to lean back into Starkad and pull his arms around her. "Now who's grumpy?" she teased. "And if Gwydion's okay with it, I don't see a problem, spoil sport."

"*I'm* the spoil sport?" Starkad bit her where neck met shoulder, leaving a delicious sting. He nipped hard in a row along her skin. "You say things like that, and I take it as a challenge." The warning in his words was disrupted by his playful tone.

Gwydion leaned into the table again, watching with a curious smirk.

Kirby covered one of Starkad's hands and slid it under her shirt, to rest on her bare stomach. "It's not a challenge if it's true." She was pushing her luck with the taunting, but that typically meant punishment. Something she was very much in favor of.

He glided his hand higher, to caress her breast through her bra. His light touch sent shivers of desire racing along her skin. The fact that they were in a public room and other people might join them any minute added to the rush.

Starkad kneaded her breast and pinched her nipple, pulling her tighter into him. His erection dug into her.

Kirby's pulse hammered in her ears and throbbed between her thighs.

As Gwydion watched, he stroked himself through his trousers.

Everything about this was deliciously wicked.

Starkad slid his other hand under the waistband of her jeans. It was a tight fit, denim biting into her hips. She didn't care, as long as everything kept feeling this good. There was no buildup or play, as he parted her folds to tease her clit.

She gasped as he traced circles around the swollen button. Her hips swayed and her eyes half-closed as his touch intensified. Climax built inside her, edging her closer to release.

"Do you really think I'm mean?" Starkad's low question rumbled through her on a hungry growl that reminded her of the wolf he could become.

She had to pull herself from pleasure, to make her mouth form words. "You're a literal sadist."

"Fair point." He pulled away, leaving disappointment and longing in its wake.

Kirby grasped the lingering corner of pleasure.

Starkad shoved two slick fingers in her mouth, letting her taste herself.

She spent several seconds on each, licking them clean and reveling in his groan.

"You're right. I always spoil the fun." He slapped her ass.

Her disappointment grew, but so did her amusement. She turned so she could see both Starkad and Gwydion. "I still have my original plan."

"I'm really up for anything." Gwydion traced a finger along her bottom lip. "Up. Eager. Hard. Waiting."

"The original plan was to convince you first, and use that as a way to tell me I was outvoted and I should give in," Starkad said.

Kirby pouted. "You're giving me far too much credit for thinking this through. It's only a battle because you're making it one. Until you said something, I'd gotten as far as, *fucking sounds like a fun distraction.*"

"But you wanted me in on it." Starkad's confidence was as sexy as the rest of him.

Kirby usually did. She enjoyed both Starkad and Gwydion separately, but *together* tended to be best.

"So if this was about the two of you, am I the backup dick?" Gwydion's tone was light and playful.

Starkad shook his head. "You're King Dick."

Did he try to make a dick joke? Their influence was rubbing off on him.

"I do like being royalty." Gwydion chuckled. "What's the next step in this intricately complicated plan that has way too many steps for its own good?"

"Later." Starkad's voice changed in an instant to that all-business snap Kirby loved in the bedroom and hated in the field.

Their guests had arrived. She knew what—whom—she was going to see when she turned around.

Still, the sight of Brit, standing next to Min in the doorway, turned her blood to ice and churned her stomach.

CHAPTER FIVE

Brit recognized Kirby's laugh halfway down the hall. That happy, musical sound Brit had elicited with ease, once upon a time.

I brought this on myself. The reminder left a bitter burn in the back of her throat.

Aeval pointed toward a doorway, and gestured for Min and Brit to enter first. Brit stalled in the entrance at the sight of Kirby, half-turned away, looking so very happy and at ease with Gwydion and Starkad.

Starkad met Brit's gaze, and his expression turned to stone. "Later," he told Kirby.

His familiar stern tone sliced through Brit. It had never meant good things for her. When Kirby faced them, Brit's heart skipped against her ribs. Time had never lessened the response, and now that Brit had severed ties with the rest of her past, she didn't feel obligated to hide her tentative smile.

Kirby's glance slid over her, but not without a flicker of recognition and... doubt?

"Hey. You made it." Gwydion's voice sounded unnaturally loud, though it was a normal volume. He crossed the room and pulled Min into a quick hug. "Good to see you again."

"You as well." Min returned the gesture.

"Everyone's here. The party can start." Kirby's voice wavered.

Aeval stepped around Brit and to the front of the room. "If there's tension here, I need to know it can be ignored or that someone is going home." She glared at Gwydion. "You promised to call people you trust."

"You're looking at everyone," Gwydion said. "It's not a long list."

Min rested a hand at Brit's back. "And I take full responsibility for her."

Brit had expected awkward, but this... This was cover-her-eyes-and-hide cringe-worthy.

"Swell." Kirby had regained her composure. She settled into a chair. "I don't have a lot of faith in who you vouch for."

Aeval swept her arm across the room. "Have a seat. Everyone, please." She didn't leave room for argument. No wonder she was a queen. A faery queen, who lived in fucking castle, in faery land. The entire scenario was amazing, and Brit had been raised by gods, so she'd seen some impressive things.

"Kirby, love, you know I adore you," Aeval continued, "but we're talking about *my* people. Their lives are at risk, and I want them back safe. That means going in with as much firepower as we can get. You." She stared at Bit. "I understand you may be immortal, but my justice isn't like theirs. If you fuck me over, there will be consequences."

Brit swore the temperature in the room dropped ten degrees. "I understand."

Min had explained to her that the fae issued retribution in the form of bad luck. Which could have some far-reaching, long term consequences.

"What do we know? The who, where—all of it," Starkad said.

Aeval gestured at the screen behind her, which flickered to life. It was almost a shame it was electrical, and not magical. A photo of an old warehouse popped up. "My people are being sold." Aeval's anger was tangible. She looked sweet and dainty, but Brit had seen her fight. She was there in the battle against Hel. "This is where the hand-off is happening. My information says they'll be here with guards, tonight."

"How many of yours are we talking about?" Kirby asked.

"Not all of them. Maybe ten, if I'm lucky." Aeval brought up the next slide—a blueprint of the building. "I can deposit us anywhere in the Earth realm. Once we find my fae, I can bring them open a gate back here, and I'll give Gwydion access to do the same."

Was this information for everyone's benefit, or was Brit the only person who didn't know it already? "How many guards?" she asked.

Aeval's frown deepened. "I don't know."

"I know that building. We both do." Kirby's animosity was gone when she turned to Brit.

Brit looked again. She'd been so distracted by everything, recognition slipped past her before. "It's an old TOM training facility." Her brain should have picked up on that immediately. Another instinct or memory lost in her temporary death. "That means three of us are familiar with it."

Starkad shook his head. "They kept me away from field training. For some reason, they never completely trusted me."

"Bad news is the structure was made for urban-warfare training. The inside layout isn't fixed beyond primary supports," Kirby said.

Gwydion drummed his fingers on the table. "Is there good news?"

"There's a lot of concrete for us to hide behind?" Brit had to reach deep for the information. Why was it so hard to access some of those bits of her life?

*

Min knew better than to expect this would be a smooth process, but Kirby and Brit's information was less than reassuring, even given the low bar.

Aeval radiated stress. He didn't blame her. TOM had taken her fae—those who served her directly, loyally, and in many cases were close friends, and were doing gods-knew-what with them.

Not notoriously kind gods, either. The members of the TOM board had earned their bloody and terrifying reputations. Hel had been brutal, but certainly wasn't at the top of the list.

"My sources indicate my people will sleep here until *buyers* are found. I assume that means at least a portion of the layout is habitable, but not necessarily comfortable," Aeval said.

"Safe assumption." Kirby was in the alert, ready-to-strike posture Min had come to associate with her in this life.

The glimpse he got of her before she knew he and Brit had arrived reminded him more of the woman he had fallen for over and over. It was good she had moments like that, even if they weren't with him.

Brit had adopted a similar posture to Kirby's—back straight and expression stony—but the last few months with her told him she was struggling with several aspects of this.

"Let's be blunt," she said. "They'll be kept functional—no physical damage, nothing that would keep them from doing whatever they're sold for. Treated like produce at the grocery store, and probably not a high-end one."

Kirby growled.

"She's right." Aeval radiated weariness. "I'm familiar with the trade for magical beings, and I'm not under any illusions that my people's fate is sunny."

"There are still kinder ways to phrase it." So Kirby did have compassion. It balanced out her training to use people's prejudices and biases against them, to shoot first and ask questions later, and to climb inside most minds and understand their perspective, regardless of how distasteful it was.

Min's perspective, on the other hand. Kirby struggled with that one.

"Any reason to put this off?" Starkad asked Aeval.

She shook her head. "My instinct is, of course, the sooner the better. When you're all rested."

"Twenty-four hours, then." Starkad moved to the front of the room, to stand next to her. "Time to rest. Prepare." He looked at Brit. "And you and I will talk."

"Sure." Brit's mask never slipped, but she paled.

Kirby stood as well. "We'll go in two teams. Aeval can plant us wherever we need, and she and Gwydion can bring us back here, so we'll split them." Gwydion could enter this realm and exit in the same place on Earth, with Aeval's blessing. "Main floor is the training room. Top floor is most likely where the fae will be kept. Team One on Level One, Team Two upstairs."

"Who else makes up each team?" Brit asked.

Starkad didn't miss a beat. "That has yet to be determined."

On the surface, it looked like Starkad and Kirby had already discussed this. Perhaps they had, but Min suspected their agreement was more a synchronicity of having worked together for many years. It was still undetermined if Brit was joining this operation.

"Team One will work its way up, Team Two down. Standard signal over the earpiece. No extraneous chatter." Kirby might be doing an effective job of ignoring Brit, but if she was discussing these plans in front of her, she believed it was all right to do so.

They finished discussing the basic plan, and Aeval excused herself.

Starkad looked at Brit. "You, Min, and I can talk in here."

"Swell." Kirby was bouncing on the balls of her feet, and had been for the last several minutes. "I'm going to go wear myself out, hitting something."

"I volunteer as tribute." Gwydion raised his hand.

Kirby almost smiled. "You don't make a great punching bag, but I've got other uses for you."

Min had never given into jealousy. However, it was impossible to ignore the envy that roared in his veins as Kirby and Gwydion left the room, arms linked and unintelligible conversation drifting from them.

There was one thing Min couldn't argue with Kirby—she wasn't the same person he'd fallen for in the past. But he saw traces of that woman and missed her. He didn't want her to change, to go back to what she'd been in former lives, but it would be nice to better get to know and understand the woman in this one.

When everyone else was gone, Starkad closed the meeting room door and took the seat directly across the table from Brit.

She stared back, jaw clenched. "What can I do for you?"

"Like I said, we're going to talk." Starkad searched her face.

Min saw the stoniness that passed between the two. He also recognized Brit's flicker of uncertainty. It wasn't obvious, but he'd spent the last six months living with her. He wasn't much of a jailer; he preferred company at meals, and conversation when she was in the mood. Which had given him plenty of time to learn the microscopic twitches that were her tells.

"How have you been?" Starkad's tone was casual, but his posture was guarded. Coiled and ready to strike at a whisper.

Brit let out a barking laugh. "*Now* you want to make small talk? More than five years, and today you care how I am?"

"You misunderstand the question," Starkad said. He wasn't concerned about her welfare; he was looking for a status update.

Min couldn't imagine having that level of callousness toward anyone.

Brit reclined in her chair and propped one foot on the table. "In that case, I'm really fucking good. I can't die. Not that living came with any sort of additional superpowers. I'm shackled to a god. Again. Still. But at least this is a nice one. Oh, and my favorite thing? I'm no longer in a place where I have to pretend it doesn't devour me to watch my girlfriend drool all over you."

"*Ex*-girlfriend." Starkad was still ice.

This conversation was deteriorating quickly.

"She was a child when she arrived on campus." The way Brit sat was deceptive. She wasn't casual or off-balance. Tension ran through her entire body.

If Starkad saw it—and why wouldn't he?—it wasn't enough to break his mask. "She's older than me."

"No. She was created before you. She has centuries-big gaps in her existence and didn't have any of those memories when we were in school."

The light twitch of Starkad's fingers against the table was the only indicator his barricade had cracked. "I never approached her."

"Until you did."

"She was dying." Starkad regained his composure. "Because you chose to save your own ass, without considering the consequences for her, and she chose the same. To save you."

The slump of Brit's shoulders dissipated a layer of the tension in the room, but the cloud still hung heavily. "I did. It was a selfish mistake I can't undo, and I'm willing to own that. Are you?"

"I can. I have. But I don't owe any of that to you."

"That's fine. Your opinion means shit to me, and I'm not here because of you any more than you want me to be here."

The verbal tennis match was fascinating, but Min saw and felt the toll it was having on Brit. She knew her situation was of her own making, but this was the first time he'd seen her bite back since she returned to life. If it was hard for Min to be this close to the woman he loved and not be able to reach out beyond casual conversation, being here had to be devouring Brit.

"Why *are* you here?" Starkad asked. "Why did you leave TOM? Why did you go back to Hel? Why are you helping now?"

Brit pursed her lips, and then her composure was back, mirroring Starkad's. "That's a lot of questions. What kind of answer are you looking for?"

"The truth."

This wasn't just two people who loved the same woman, taking shots at each other. Starkad was probing Brit's edges to see how she delivered the answers. Because it was always about the game here. Keeping up the lie. Seeing who cracked first.

Did it ever end?

"From the top. I left TOM because I was a selfish child who thought I was owed better." Brit held out her hand and extended her index finger. "I went back to Hel because I hate her and wanted to help in her death." She ticked up another finger. "And yeah, I did it for Kirby, too. Whether or not anyone believes me. And I'm here now because... what else am I going to do?" Instead of extending a third finger, she retracted the first, flipping off Starkad.

Starkad rolled his eyes. "Boredom doesn't make for the most stable motivation."

"Sorry we can't all have centuries of obsession to drive us. The people you work with are pursuing the thing I hate. I don't have a lot of marketable skills, and I sure as fuck don't have a past to fall back on, to get a *normal* job. You think I'd pass any background check for a security job? I could go be a high-priced call girl, except I promised myself I'd die before I ever fucked anyone again that I didn't want to. Since I probably can't die…"

"*Nothing* new besides the not-being-able-to-die thing?" Starkad asked. "No trace of the power Hel gave you?"

Brit scrubbed her face and planted both feet on the floor. "Haven't had a lot of chance to test if I can fly or anything, but no. Kind of faster healing. Same amount of pain. Can't move any quicker. Can't lift anything heavy. Still short."

Starkad studied her. An awkward silence descended in the room.

"No more questions, then?" Irritation bled from Brit's voice, and she stood. "No more seeing how much truth I'm willing to give you?"

Starkad didn't respond.

CHAPTER SIX

Kirby dug her toes into the workout mat, as she faced Gwydion. Her posture was casual. His was more guarded.

In a way, Aeval's castle reminded Kirby of the TOM campus, where she was trained and raised. But the atmosphere here was warmer. Kinder.

She needed to burn off a lot excess energy— more than sex would take care of—so she was sparring with Gwydion in one of the training rooms. A thin sheen of sweat clung to her skin, and portions of her ached from exertion and his hits. It was perfect.

"You look tired." He bounced on the balls of his feet. "You sure you want another round?"

"Absolutely." She kept her tone as easygoing as her stance, but she never took her eyes off the way he moved. Even if Starkad weren't talking to Brit, Kirby didn't spar with him anymore. Because he'd trained her in this life and they'd practiced together so frequently since, they spent more time watching each other, waiting for someone to twitch, than they did actually throwing any strikes.

Gwydion moved first, as was typical of these sessions, stepping in with a feint of a right hook, that blended into a knee where he hoped her leg would land as she dodged.

Kirby sidestepped both, but tripped on a root that had magically appeared in her path, in the middle of the mat. She recovered, and the obstruction vanished. The kick she directed at the back of Gwydion's knee landed solidly.

He grunted, rolling as he hit the mat and coming back up on his feet. He faced her again, playful grin in place and loose fists up. "Predictable."

"You're one to talk." Kirby landed a fist in his gut with enough impact to force him back a step. The words were more taunt than truth. She'd become familiar with some of his go-to moves, but he surprised her on a regular basis.

Gwydion wasn't trained in any specific fighting style. He was a brawler with centuries of experience, the strength of a god, and magic. He was also good at ducking and weaving. What looked like over-correcting for his stumble turned into a roll. He swept a leg out into hers.

She jumped. The root appeared as her feet left the ground, not giving her any out but to land on it or adjust her stance. She managed a bit of both, but still lost her balance.

Gwydion straddled her, pinning her to the mat, and dipped his head to brush his lips over hers.

Another thing she loved about sparring with him—he didn't take it nearly as seriously as most people. She leaned into the kiss, focused both on the weight of his body and on her next move to twist out from under him.

He pinned her wrists above her head before she could move, stealing her leverage and locking her in place.

Kirby laughed. "You win. You cheated, but you win."

"How did I cheat?" His grin was broad. He trailed his lips along her neck.

Pleasant shivers raced over her, and she tilted her head, to give him better access. She sighed at the playful attention. "Sorry—what?"

"How did I cheat?" His lips vibrated against her skin.

He hadn't. There were no rules beyond those they imposed on themselves. Typically, he didn't use his full strength, and she didn't summon her magical shield.

Gwydion traveled his mouth lower, along her collarbone.

Kirby groaned. "I'm thinking *raw sex appeal.*"

"That's cheating now?" He pulled back to meet her gaze. His grin matched hers. "Because I can't turn it off."

She shifted her weight, grinding her hips up into him, looking for a new distraction to give her the advantage. Not that she minded this.

He tightened his grip on her wrists. "Fool me once, shame on you. Fool me sixty-nine times—"

"*Sixty-nine?* Really?" She snorted.

The sound of Starkad clearing his throat reached them. If he were alone, he'd be watching or joining in, so there was a reason he was interrupting.

Brit's heavy sigh followed, and Kirby's good mood evaporated.

Gwydion pressed his mouth to Kirby's ear. "I could bind and gag her with branches," he whispered. "Buy a couple more minutes."

"Are you trying to make me jealous? Don't you dare." Kirby felt better at the teasing.

Gwydion gave her another kiss, this one sweetly chaste on the cheek, and helped her to her feet.

Starkad, Min, and Brit stood at the edge of the mats. Kirby could almost hear the sarcastic, *Sorry to interrupt*, racing through Brit's thoughts and matching her scowl.

Brit's expression was oddly comforting. If she were trying to hide her irritation, Kirby would be more suspicious.

"I'm sorry to interrupt." Starkad's apology was genuine. "We'd like to gauge what Brit can do. Are you up for finding out?"

"We know what I can do." Frustration filled Brit's reply. "Coming back to life didn't give me anything new but the ability to come back to life."

So she said. If Starkad thought Brit was a significant threat, he wouldn't be proposing this.

"Wouldn't you rather fight someone who doesn't know all your moves?" Kirby asked.

Brit smirked. "You haven't seen me fight in almost six years. I promise, you don't know them all."

This was different—the confidence, the lack of deference. Very unlike the Brit who blamed Kirby for most of her problems.

Kirby stepped forward. "Spread 'em."

Brit placed her feet shoulder-width apart, and her arms straight out at her sides.

Kirby patted her down for weapons.

"You're making it too easy to grab the one-liners," Brit quipped. "I know you like an audience—"

"And I know your go-to move is *stab an ally in the back*." Kirby didn't want to fall into any sort of banter with Brit.

"Touché."

"Am I allowed to voice my concern?" Gwydion asked. He'd joined the other men at the edge of the mat.

Starkad shook his head. "No. But you are allowed—"

"He's not." Kirby knew where that thought was going. It would sound something like, *You* are *allowed to step in if things go wrong.* "You want to see this? Then watch. Don't interfere."

Brit's smirk grew.

Kirby stepped back onto the mat and gestured for Brit to join her. The stare-down was similar to the start of most of Kirby's sparring matches, but Brit had never been patient.

Kirby twitched.

Brit attacked with a swinging kick, aimed at Kirby's shins.

Kirby stepped out of range, but Brit pressed the attack, throwing one punch, then a second.

Kirby dodged. She countered with a spinning kick at Brit's head.

Brit ducked under Kirby's leg and bounced on her toes, waiting. "You don't have to pull your punches. You're not going to hurt me any more than he did." She nodded at Min.

"I could say the same to you." Kirby launched a gut punch and connected.

Brit leaned into the attack and threw a one-two jab.

Kirby blocked both.

"That thing G does, with the roots growing out of the ground..." Brit kneed Kirby in the gut.

Kirby deflected most of the impact. "Neat, right?" How did Gwydion feel about the nickname? He was probably a lot more okay with it than Starkad would be if someone called him *S*. "I can have him toss a couple more in here. Mix things up."

"That sounds distinctly like the interfering you told them not to do," Brit said. "Are one too many trips over those roots the reason you favor your left leg?" Her straight punch connected solidly with Kirby's cheekbone, sending sparkles of pain through her.

Kirby exaggerated her stumble. "That's not real. I want you to think the leg is weak."

"Telling me defeats the purpose, and fighting that way keeps you off balance. I call *bullshit*." Brit circled Kirby.

Kirby studied her movements, watching and waiting for the right cue. "Call it what you want. Your opinion doesn't change reality."

Brit targeted Kirby's leg with a sweep of her own.

Kirby pushed off the *bad* leg, into a spinning kick that caught Brit in the chest and knocked her to her ass.

She was on her feet again before Kirby touched the ground.

"You still prefer grappling on the mat?" Kirby kicked.

Brit dropped her arms, to block. "Only with the right person. You volunteering?" There was no animosity in her retort.

Kirby was enjoying this. Not just the workout, but also the banter she'd wanted to avoid. The playful feeling could be because she and Brit were psychically taking their frustrations out on each other, but this exchange was fun. Perish the thought she might enjoy her time with Brit. "I'm good up here, thanks." She swung her elbow at Brit's jaw.

Brit rolled with the hit, grabbed Kirby's wrist, and twisted. "You've never complained about tumbling with me before."

"These days, I have a much better idea of how I like to be hurt." Kirby broke the grip and bounced back to throw her body weight into another kick.

Brit dodged. "You and me both."

"Mariah Carey still?" Kirby executed a flurry of smaller kicks and chopped her arm toward Brit's neck.

Brit blocked and punched over her own block. "Too much *ouch* there. But she's better than Taylor Swift."

Time to wrap this up. Kirby ducked, to drive her shoulder into Brit's gut, and pushed her back until she collided with a padded support. "Taylor Swift wishes she could write breakup songs about me." Kirby didn't mean the words cruelly, but would they set Brit off?

"She wouldn't do you justice." Brit's retort was breathless, but calm. She pummeled her fists into Kirby's sides.

Kirby returned the punches, pushing away before she took too many herself. She bounced on the balls of her feet. Where to strike next? "I should probably counter something like that with something cheesy, about being the one who delivers justice."

"You should probably counter with your left forearm."

Kirby raised her right one instead. When Brit struck her exactly where she'd warned, it left Kirby's head ringing.

Now they both knew that trick. She drove her shoulder into Brit's stomach again.

Brit rolled with the attack, reaching over her head, to grab the support pillar. She picked her legs off the ground, wrapped them around Kirby's neck, and dropped both women to the mat.

Brit's chokehold on Kirby was anything but playful, threatening to cut off her air supply.

Kirby had her fist rested at Brit's side, though. "It's a draw if you're lucky." She rasped the words.

"You don't have a weapon or leverage, and as long as I choke you before you twist free, I win." Brit squeezed her thigh harder.

Kirby tapped the mat, and Brit moved. Relief filtered through Kirby, as she gasped for breath. She rolled onto her side and slammed her fist into the mat. A hole burned through the padding, and a small crater exploded around her attack. That was new. A glance at the men showed their surprise.

Kirby hid hers. "It's a draw." What else could she learn, with Brit pushing her in sparring? Carelessness, probably.

Brit rolled onto her knees. "It's a draw." She stood and offered Kirby a hand.

Kirby didn't hesitate to accept the offer of help up. This was more fun than she expected. Too bad it couldn't happen again—the thought pinged with regret in her chest. "You've gotten better."

A smile ghosted across Brit's face. "So have you. Who do I have to fuck to get myself a Super Sayan Fist of Doom like that?"

"Odin." Kirby didn't want to be having fun. More than the challenge of the fight sped through her veins. Brit's company was nice. Possibly even pleasantly enjoyable.

Brit furrowed her brow. "I mean, I suppose if I had to. Nope. Still wouldn't do it."

"I don't recommend it anyway." Kirby stopped a light laugh from slipping out, and gave her attention to Starkad. "Verdict?" Not just about the fight, but also the mission, the pairings—all of it.

"Team One—Aeval, you, and me. Team Two—Brit, Gwydion, and Min." Starkad's answer provided much more information than a list of names.

It was expected that Gwydion and Aeval would split up. The rest of the pairing offs meant Starkad trusted Brit enough to do what she was trained for, but not so much that she could be unsupervised. And if she did become an issue, Min would disable her, and Gwydion would still be fire-support.

It also meant Starkad didn't want Kirby and Brit paired. A reasonable decision, based on their skills, and a potent reminder that to him, Brit was barely more than a dangerously useful weapon.

Kirby glanced at Brit, and for a heartbeat, the woman looking back was the person Kirby had fallen in love with and done everything to protect.

A sharp pain jabbed through her chest—the ghost of a wound she'd never actually received, from a bullet fired at her hundreds of times, by Brit. It was a potent reminder of where they stood now.

"I agree," Kirby said to Starkad.

Brit chuckled dryly. Would she protest? She shrugged. "Better than I expected. And a lot better than being locked in my room."

CHAPTER SEVEN

For the first time in many months, Min could allow himself the full freedom to relax. Everyone was staying in Aeval's fortress, in preparation for tomorrow's mission.

He rarely slept, but he sought rest and recovery in the form of a meditation that allowed his mind to flow where it would and process the world around him.

Tonight, his mind lulled him gently toward a moment more than two-thousand years ago, in his own palace.

Intricately carved stone spread around him, racing in pillars toward the sky, and flowing into benches and steps. Magically lit torches lined the walls, casting sensuous shadows around the bodies that filled the room.

Dozens of people in various stages of undress writhed in pleasure. With each other, with themselves, and in hopes of drawing his attention.

This celebration of life and fertility was a tribute to him. In return, he'd influence the harvests and the births, and tonight he'd bestow his grace on a few who caught his eye.

He sat on his throne, surveying his believers. Feeling as much as seeing, the passion that flowed through the room.

Some of the gods operated out of spite—if they didn't get what they wanted, they ensured their followers suffered. Min preferred to offer pleasure—his and theirs—in exchange for worship.

Amid the undulating flesh, one body captured his gaze. So pale, she almost glowed against the dark skin around her. He'd met with paler-skinned peoples, though he wasn't a fan of most of the Greek gods who chose to masquerade as Roman, rather than own their origins.

However, this woman was statuesque marble. Her skin, her hair, and her eyes were alabaster. One of those Greek statues, brought to life, including the lightweight shift that covered but didn't hide ample breasts and hips.

She fixed her gaze on his and strolled toward him, a sensuous sway to her hips and a confident smile on her lips. The crowds parted around her. As she reached the platform his throne sat on, she never bowed in deference.

New and tempting. "What can I bestow upon you this evening?" he asked.

"Your adoration." Mischief tickled her smile.

The same thing so many others wanted. "I don't offer that to just anyone, but you're intriguing," he said. "What's your name?"

"Urd." Rather than kneeling at the base of the steps leading to him, the way his followers did, she approached until she stood next to him. "And tonight, you will worship me. It's written in the stars."

Amusement tickled his senses, and he rose. No one towered over him. Desire flitted across his tongue, wanting to know how this marble creature, who thought she could stand on his ground without humility, would taste. "What else do the stars say?"

Urd pressed her body closer and crooked her finger, motioning for him to lower his head. She brushed her mouth over his ear. "They tell me not to give you the important information until you've proven to me why these people all worship you," she whispered. "Until you've knelt at my feet and shown me true pleasure."

Min didn't kneel before anyone, including his brothers and sisters. He was also loathe to refuse such a succulent challenge. He tore her dress away, and offered her everything she requested and more. The room felt the swell of his passion and the climax of hers. Many times.

She stayed with him through the night, along with others he'd graced with his glory. Half a dozen people lay tangled together in his bed, when he awoke the next morning.

He left his devoted followers and his clothes behind, to step outside and greet the sunrise. The sand and native grasses were soft and warm against the bare soles of his feet.

Urd joined him. The predawn light cast her nude form in a pale pink glow. Today she was quartz, and just as stunning. "When the visions come to me, they're impressions. Words. No emotion. If I were to feel them." She shuddered. "What you showed me last night was a moment I only wish to live once. It was so glorious, I'm grateful I experienced it firsthand and not through a flash of images."

Of course her time with him had been glorious. "What else have you seen?" Min asked. Some oracles were truly gifted, and others were looking to deceive. Urd radiated truth, but that simply meant she believed the things she said, not that they were true prophecy.

"So many things. People you'll meet. Others you never will. You. Falling in love. Losing her. Many times. A pale beauty whom you'll offer a greater devotion than your followers give you."

Tying himself to one person? Ridiculous thought. "I suppose this is where you tell me *you're* that pale beauty."

"Me?" Urd's crystal laugh matched her celestial appearance. "No. If you and I are to ever meet again, the stars refuse to tell me. She'll never have to demand your adoration. You'll offer it freely. She's your equal and opposite. Your greatest weakness and your most potent strength. And neither of you will achieve your full potential without the other."

"I'll never bind myself to one individual. Not with the completeness you're describing."

Urd stepped in front of him, to hold his gaze. "Neither will she. But you'll worship her and bow before her, and she'll offer the same in return."

Min snapped himself from the deep meditation, and his current room swam back into view. The moment he met Urd was distinct and potent, living under his skin as if he'd experienced it now, and not centuries ago.

The encounter was the reason he followed her prophecies even now, but the specifics of their meeting had faded from his memory long before he met Kirby.

Everyone familiar with Urd's prophecies had a different opinion on how real they were, but Min knew she'd written each with a true gift. The gift of fate. The ability to follow the threads of time and unravel them.

It was tempting to wander nude into the moonlight and feel the world on his skin.

This was a different time. A different place. He pulled on a pair of lightweight muslin bottoms and wandered into the castle hallway.

*

How long would Kirby be addicted to the night-before-a-mission schedule she learned with TOM? Forcing sleep with the help of medication. Forcing consciousness with a different pill. And letting adrenaline keep her awake until then.

Her being awake took care of another nagging thought, though. She hadn't needed long, to adjust to sharing a bed with Starkad and Gwydion. It felt more right than most things in her life. But there was still an ache that something—someone—was missing. It didn't help that every place Aeval owned had ridiculously huge beds.

Kirby needed to burn excess energy. Not too long ago, that need meant hooking up with a random person in a hotel bar. If she wanted to get laid tonight, Gwydion would be her distraction. But right now he was digging up information about the god they'd run into—Finn—and Starkad was working some contacts, to glean any last-minute information about the mission.

So Kirby was strolling through marble-and-stone hallways, on beautifully woven rugs, not appreciating the wonder of the castle nearly as much as it deserved.

Seeing Brit today was odd. Infuriating, but fun. It was wreaking havoc on Kirby's thoughts. There was no universe where Brit could be forgiven for what she'd done. She'd have to do something drastic, like sacrifice herself to save someone else, to prove her remorse.

And she had. Now she was a prisoner. One with looser boundaries than during her time with TOM, but she still didn't have the freedom she'd wanted.

Kirby needed to put those thoughts aside until the mission was over. Then things would go back to the way they were. Brit would be back with Min.

And Kirby wouldn't.

As if summoned by her thoughts, he was striding down the hallway when she turned the corner.

His dark beauty amid the palace's pale splendor made Kirby's heart skip. His smile when he saw her was sunshine cascading over her skin. "Hunt— Kirby. Do you have a moment?"

"Yes." The answer came easily. She didn't know what else to say, but she was happy to see him.

He approached until he was close enough to reach out and touch her. "I'm sorry."

Her brain stalled at the apology. "Oh?"

"I can't apologize for loving you. I don't regret that, and I still feel it. When I found out what Daz had done—betraying you to Hel—I obliterated him without hesitation. That moment shifted my perspective. I have a better idea now why you pursued Hel. I'm sorry I was unable to see it sooner."

His sincere words bathed her in uncertainty, making it even more difficult to find her own response. "I'm sorry I asked you to leave." It slipped out before she could consider the implications. "I mean, I don't regret it, but."

Min turned, forcing her to do the same, to hold his gaze, and he took another step toward her. The wall was at her back, keeping her from moving away. She should be furious with his cornering her, and she knew half a dozen ways to move him by force in the next half a second, that he'd never see coming.

Instead, her heart slammed against her ribs like she was a scared rabbit, and a desire that belonged to a past version of her raced through her veins. Her mind, heart, and body all wanted very different things from this man—this god—and logic was rapidly losing ground.

Was that such a bad thing?

"But…?" Min prompted.

"I'm still making sense of it. I'm glad you're here."

He cupped her cheek, and ghosts of familiarity sparked between then. "As am I." His voice was deep. Seductive. He leaned in until his lips hovered millimeters from hers, his warm breath teasing her skin. "And now that I am, I intend to meet your challenge."

"Which one?" Her question came out as a squeak.

He trailed his thumb along her jawline. "You deserve to be worshiped—you won't change my mind about that. And I'm going to remind you why we always fall in love." His kiss was so light, she felt the intent as much as the sensation.

Kirby's pulse hammered in her ears. Her breath came in shallow pants, and her imagination raced with a vivid blend of memory and fantasy.

"Sleep well, Huntress. And be safe. We have a lot of missed time to make up for when this is over." Min stepped away.

The cool air that rushed in around Kirby didn't do anything to soothe her out-of-control desire.

CHAPTER EIGHT

Starkad was first through the portal Aeval opened onto the top floor of the warehouse. It was like walking through a door into a new room. A potentially heavily guarded room. He cleared corners and blind spots—not that there was much of either in here—in what looked like it had once been an office.

He aimed himself and his Desert Eagle .40 at the only door in the room, and waved Kirby in. She set herself next to the door with her back to the wall. The windowless room was the farthest from the stairs, and would become their fallback locale if needed. The position served as a solid starting point for a search, and the single doorway would be a funnel for TOM soldiers if this group came under attack and needed to hold this position.

Aeval came through last, closing her magical gate behind her. She looked harmless, but she could summon storms from the skies and had access to magics not even the gods could wield.

Starkad met Kirby's gaze, and she gave a terse nod. *Ready*. Time to move to the next room.

The hallway was empty. It was nerve-wracking, to be up here without cover, but that also meant nothing for their opponents to hide behind. The only indicator this place had been used recently was the lack of dust—also good. Starkad's group wouldn't leave footprints, making it easier to hide where they'd been and where they were going.

The second room was as empty as the first— a box with four walls, no furniture, and a tiny closet. The next few rooms were the same.

Starkad had never been in this particular building, but the concept was straightforward. It was a gutted warehouse, with offices upstairs and open space downstairs. When the place was in use, the offices were as much a part of the urban-warfare training as everything else. Today, every single one had to be cleared, to make sure nothing—no one— was missed.

With each empty room, the tension in the air dialed a little higher. Where were Aeval's people? She should be able to sense them, but she hadn't given them a direction. Their presence may be masked from her.

The silence set his nerves on edge, and his wolf whined to get out. This was a battlefield. Whispers of gunpowder and blood hung in the air. Most people would run, but his berserker wanted to fight. The lack of an enemy was the biggest issue. Each scuff of shoes on the floor, each breath, was another sound for him to focus on. Did the sounds come from his people or TOM's?

He sensed Kirby, as he had since the fight with Hel. She was at his side and had his back. Few thoughts were more comforting.

Another empty room. More silence on the radio. An extra notch of tension.

Starkad hadn't wanted to bring Brit. He'd prefer she stay as far away from them as possible. Min vouched for her, but Starkad had lost all faith in Min's judgment when it came to people and the lies they told.

One thing Starkad believed without question—Brit would always serve her own interests. When she'd reached out, years ago, offering inside information about TOM, Starkad spent several months vetting her intel. Not that he ever told her that. He let her think he trusted her from the start.

He'd intended to continue eliminating TOM assassins on his own, and he only brought Kirby in when she begged for a way to make up for her past. When he saw another path to help her heal.

Min felt Brit was dropping her guard. That she'd stopped wearing the mask TOM indoctrinated her with. Starkad had been watching her deteriorate into this for years. He believed she was desperate to get out. That she'd *sworn loyalty* to Hel in order to kill the goddess and secure an exit. And he believed that Brit thought she loved Kirby.

However, he didn't know what Brit's final goal was, and that worried him.

Three more rooms down, and not many left to go. Something was wrong. They had two options—keep pushing forward, or retreat and try again later. Falling back wasn't a real choice. Not until they *knew* this place was empty.

Teeth gnashed inside his head, needing something to latch onto.

The sparring session between Brit and Kirby yesterday was more telling than any words. If Brit had been holding back, she'd become the most incredible fighter and actress in the universe. She'd never been able to beat back her urge to best Kirby at something. She'd given that fight her all. Any claims she made about not having any new power or magic seemed legitimate.

Starkad, Kirby, and Aeval were almost at the end of the floor. The stairs and one final room loomed before them. Did Brit sell them out? The possibility was slim. She'd been accompanied since she arrived at Aeval's. Surrounded by heavy wards and even heavier observation. And it was unlikely she had access to the information Aeval did before it was distributed.

So where were the fae? Their guards?

As they pushed into the last empty room, Kirby stepped up next to him with a worried glance. *Behind us.* Danger howled in his skull.

Gunshots rang out from downstairs. Starkad pressed Aeval against a wall in the room, and he and Kirby took up similar positions. If anyone came in here, the new arrivals would be targets. But TOM knew better than to walk through a bottleneck like that. It also meant if anyone tried to leave the room, they'd be just as easy to hit.

"My people are here," Aeval whispered. "They weren't before."

They could get out of here quickly, then. "We need a portal out of here, and another into the room where they."

Aeval shook her head. "I'm trying. Something is keeping me from summoning an exit."

"We can fight our way down to them, but if you can't open a portal, what are we supposed to do when we get there?" Kirby kept her gaze on the door, and there was no emotion in her voice.

She didn't need to let her worry show for Starkad to recognize it. He felt the same. "We'll deal with it when we get there." Now was a bad time to stop and plan. If they killed the opposition, they could walk out the front door.

If.
*

This wasn't right. In fact, there was nothing about the situation that Brit liked. The bottom floor was empty. If prisoners—merchandise—we being kept here, her team should have encountered guards stationed at the entrances, the staircases, and in strategic sniper positions.

She took lead, to clear the few rooms and hidden spaces down here. She hadn't taken this position since she worked with Kirby, and she'd never been comfortable as a spotter. She wanted to watch the world through her scope, where she could see the trouble coming from a distance, and take it out with a single twitch of her trigger finger. But she was an expendable body in this group. That wasn't a secret.

Something lingered in the air. The same sensation that crawled over her when they'd approached the potential's home. It crawled over her skin and coated her tongue with memories of the TOM campus she was raised on. She'd never been able to feel this tangible, gritty sensation before a few days ago.

Min didn't belong here. Sure, bullets weren't a big deal for him, and someone had to keep her in check, but his being a non-combatant made her feel responsible for him. It was another piece dividing her attention.

Gwydion should have been okay. He'd been a soldier. But he was radiating something that bordered on panic, and the sensation clawed at Brit's veins.

What the fuck kind of team had she been saddled with? If Starkad wanted to destroy her, there were easier ways.

Brit's body coiled like a compressed spring, and alarms sounded in her skull. "*Get down*," she hissed as she whirled.

A muzzle flashed in the distance, accompanied by gunfire. How did she see that? She dove for what little cover she could find, behind a half-wall near a staircase. Gwydion and Min had hidden. Good.

She fired at the spot the shot came from, and ducked. Two more bullets bit the concrete in front of her, spraying shrapnel.

"What's going on?" Starkad barked in her earpiece.

"Busy. Take a guess." The neurons in her brain were working overtime, trying to point her attention in one direction or another. If she focused, she lost the lead. She had to let the feeling wash over her and guide her attention.

She fired another shot, purely on instinct, then turned to Min and Gwydion. "One of you two can do something?"

"Not any faster than you can." Gwydion scanned the room, gun drawn. At least he hadn't given into the fear bubbling inside him. "Anything I do that impacts the area will us as well. And the building is metal and concrete. I need wood."

Another time and place, Brit would have taken the opportunity to make a joke. Now, she kept her attention on their surroundings. "We're all immortal here. Min, that thing you do to me..." That felt like it was searing the flesh from her bones and made her scream in agony.

"We're not all immortal in the same way, and not all of Aeval's people are."

Brit could argue this later. She should have brought it up before they stepped into the building, but this mission was supposed to be like any other. Where did things go wrong? She could ask that all day and cast blame in a lot of places, but it didn't get them out of here.

"They're down there." Aeval's voice hummed in Brit's ear. "My people. They're near the exterior. Whatever was hiding them has stopped, but I can't get us down there."

Of course. No reason to mask their presence, with the open gunfire. Gwydion could only enter and exit Aeval's realm from the same spot on Earth, which meant he couldn't create a gate out of here before the mission objectives were complete. Everything about this situation was fucked.

And Brit felt more alive and like she belonged than she had since she died. "I need eyes," she barked at Gwydion. "Which direction?"

"North quadrant, Room Charlie." Kirby's voice was in her ear.

Just like old times. But with more animosity and less threat of sexual assault back home.

"Min, fall back first. Gwydion give me targets. I'll cover you and follow last." Brit was using too many words. Taking too long. If Kirby were down here, this much talking wouldn't be required.

Min sprinted across the warehouse. Movement caught Brit's eye, and she fired before the soldier hiding in the shadows could get a shot off. Another bullet bit into the ground, in front of Min's feet, and Brit caught the source, fired, and hit her mark.

Gunfire sounded behind her. Some was Gwydion's, and some farther away. What good was having a god fighting by her side, if he couldn't use his magic?

But TOM knew this place would limit his powers. The warehouse was laid out and stripped down, to keep him from being effective.

She caught sight of the people targeting him, and picked off the first one. "*Go,*" she barked.

Gwydion took off, running.

"We're working out way down to you, but we're pinned." Kirby's out-of-breath words crackled in Brit's ear. "No ETA."

Because of course.

TOM might not have planned on two teams, but they'd done an effective job of keeping the groups separated. At least Kirby and Starkad had each other. Brit's jealousy had nothing to do with their romance, and everything to do with a practiced team, watching each other's backs.

Brit eliminated another shooter and followed Gwydion to the room Kirby had indicated.

He was sending the last fae through his portal. She thought those weren't working?

They could get out of here. Brit opened her mouth to call *all clear*.

"There's one more," Aeval said.

Fuck. "Where?"

Silence. Brit gritted her teeth. The gunfire on the main floor had stopped, but it still echoed from up above.

"Two doors down. Room Echo," Kirby finally responded.

Brit stepped up to the doorway. It was safe in here. "Wait until I give the *all clear*," she said. She risked a step outside the room. When no shots greeted her, she bolted to the spot Kirby indicated.

She burst through the door, weapon drawn, and pulled up short when she saw a soldier with a gun pressed to his prisoner's head.

The soldier looked at Brit, eyes wide. "You're back," he whispered. "So it's true. The faithful will return."

"Yeah. Great." Brit aimed, fired, and the soldier directly between the eyes.

"For Death," a man behind her said.

At the sound of another gunshot, Brit's world went black.

CHAPTER NINE

Kirby and Starkad held their position until they received the *All Clear* from Aeval and Gwydion. Kirby hated walking out of that building without any fae behind them, but if the other team got everyone, that was what mattered.

The knowledge didn't stop the crawling over Kirby's skin that something was wrong.

Aeval opened the portal back to her realm without issue. Go figure. Which god could block someone else from accessing their full magic? A question to figure out when they weren't still in a war zone.

Aeval, Kirby, and Starkad left the eerie silence of the warehouse behind.

They stepped into a hospital ward in Aeval's palace, where her people were huddled. Aeval rushed to their side, and a chorus of sighs accompanied hugs and chatter.

Gwydion's portal was still open—a shimmering doorway with near-zero visibility to the other side. Where were he and his team?

Min stepped through, Brit cradled in his arms and Gwydion by his side.

An unwilling sob escaped Kirby's throat, and she rushed forward. All she saw was them. Brit lay limp and lifeless, a glaring red hole in her throat with fresh blood spilling from the wound and clotting in an ugly stain on her body.

Instinct lingered at the surface, driving Kirby's actions. She brushed her fingers over Brit's cheek, focusing healing energy on the contact.

Her magic collided with an invisible wall and rushed back into her, like a jolt of adrenaline. Like she needed more of that right now.

"I need equipment." Gwydion's sharp tone yanked Kirby from her thoughts.

Aeval looked up from her reunion, and shock spread across her face. "Follow me."

They spilled into the hallway and traveled down a few doors.

"You two stay here." Gwydion looked at Kirby and Starkad. "Min, with me."

Kirby wanted to protest, but apparently she couldn't help. She planted her back against a nearby wall and slid to the ground. Her thoughts were too numb to even touch questions like, *How will I feel if she's dead this time*?

"Hey." Starkad crouched in front of her.

"I swear, if you say something like *Mission Accomplished*, I'll smack you."

He rested his hands on her knees. "I'm not your combat instructor. I'm your lover."

"Thanks for the update, asshole." Seriously. What the fuck?

He gave her a dry smile. "It doesn't matter how much certain parts of the palace look like campus; this isn't TOM. You're safe here, and Brit won't find better treatment anywhere in the world."

The words wrapped themselves into a lump in Kirby's throat, and she swallowed the reassurance she hadn't realized she needed. She recognized Brit's wound. If a soldier was going to shoot someone in the back of the head at point-blank range, they'd do it at the base of the neck. No skull. Better chance for a kill shot. "That's the kind of injury no one is supposed to recover from."

"Brit's not *no one*. She survived the wrath of a god." Starkad sat next to Kirby and tugged her to sit on his outstretched legs.

Kirby rested her head on his chest. "Thank you." She'd sort out her feelings later. Maybe go back to wishing Brit dead, once Gwydion confirmed she was going to live.

How long could Kirby sit here with Starkad, before their legs went numb?

The door next to them opened much sooner than she expected. Half an hour maybe? That couldn't be a good sign. Her stomach bottomed out, and she looked up at Gwydion. *She's gone.* His voice was already echoing in her thoughts.

"She's alive." Gwydion offered Kirby a hand and tugged her to her feet. "X-Rays fifteen minutes apart show the damage is healing. I suspect she'll be fine in about twelve hours."

Kirby almost choked on a laugh of relief. "All on her own?"

"As far as I can tell. If you're going to hang around, do so in her room. There are chairs in there." Gwydion looked at Starkad. "Not you, though. At least let the wounds heal before you turn that glower on her."

"Fine." Starkad kissed Kirby on the forehead and squeezed her hand. "Will you be all right?"

Kirby nodded. "I'm not the one with a hole in my neck." The gaping chasm of confusion in her heart wasn't the same.

She followed Gwydion into the room, where Brit lay in the sole bed. Machines surrounded her, but she was only hooked up to a vital-sign monitor, which beeped contentedly with a regular pulse and heartbeat.

A sheet covered Brit, the pale blue drawing out the translucence in her skin and making her look like she was cast from ice.

Kirby's mind was chaos that refused to use words. A jumble of jagged edges she couldn't vocalize beyond a frustrated scream. So she bit it all back. "Where's Min?"

"He went to change." Gwydion nodded at another door in the room.

Right. Because he'd been covered in blood. Brit's blood. Kirby looked at the motionless body again. The dark red, clotted and clinging to her skin. "You haven't cleaned her up."

"That's next. Diagnosis was most important, and then telling you. She's going to sleep for a while, either way."

"May I?" Kirby winced at her own question. Did she want that kind of contact? It was medical. Nothing more.

Gwydion nodded and pointed her toward sterile water and sponges.

Kirby wiped away the dried gore from Brit's skin as gently as she could. So many people had their lives cut short, by disease, outside forces, or even themselves. Why did some get so many chances? Kirby'd had more than a dozen, and now Brit was on Number Three.

Two people trained to end lives, who kept getting extras in return.

Kirby shook the thought aside before it could creep toward the shadows that always lived in the back of her mind.

When she finished cleaning Brit, she covered her with a robe and settled into a chair to wait.

Gwydion stayed as well, monitoring Brit's vitals and holding Kirby's hand.

Aeval stopped in, to shower them with gratitude for returning so many of her people. Kirby and everyone else involved in the rescue were welcome in Aeval's palace for as long as they wanted or needed to stay, with an open invitation to return whenever they needed.

For the next four or five hours, Gwydion sat with Kirby, waiting. He checked Brit's bandages occasionally, removing them when the flesh had knitted together, leaving fresh, bright-pink skin where the wound had been.

"She's going to wake up soon. She shouldn't speak yet, though," Gwydion said.

Kirby nodded. The news didn't offer relief or disappointment, just more ambivalence. "They knew we were coming." Her words tumbled out. It figured that was where her mind would arrange itself first. Who needed to focus on the emotional, when there was a mission gone bad to pick apart? "Not just one of us. They chose that location, and staged it to stifle most of the skills we'd have on our team." The addition of a second TOM trained sniper, Brit, may have been the only variable they didn't account for.

"Aeval vetted that intel. I guarantee you."

Casting blame could masquerade as catharsis, but it didn't offer solutions. "It doesn't matter. The longer we wait for something to do with TOM—for a lead, for a direction—the more likely that information will be another setup like this."

"What do you propose?" Gwydion asked.

"I don't know." Kirby's frustration puffed out in a ball of uselessness. Her gaze landed on Brit again. "Thank you for taking care of her."

The door opened and closed on a whisper, and Starkad stepped into the room. His presence was calming, which meant he wasn't here with bad news.

Gwydion rose to check Brit's wounds again. It was a brief examination. Not much to see at this point. "She was a soldier through and through in there. She didn't hesitate to shoot or react."

"That's the wonder of the training," Starkad said. "Drilled into them until it becomes instinct."

His tone rubbed Kirby wrong. Or maybe it was the words. He wasn't only talking about Brit. "So is self-preservation. But she knew taking that shot would get her killed."

"You would have done the same." Gwydion's response was what Kirby wanted to hear, but it wasn't comforting.

"Self-preservation is at the core of what Brit does," Starkad said.

Unlike Kirby. The unspoken second half of his statement echoed in her head regardless. Her selflessness wasn't bad, except... Was she doing it for any better reason than Brit? Just a year ago, Kirby would have taken that same shot to taunt death. Now she didn't know how she would react.

"That's my point." Gwydion lingered near the bed and crossed his arms. "She was there for us. For the mission. Not for herself. Min is right about her."

Was he? The single question jarred loose the rest of Kirby's jumbled thoughts. Brit didn't act this way. She didn't rush in. She didn't shoot at the risk of sacrificing herself.

"You can't say that with certainty. None of you knows her." Kirby looked at Starkad. "Especially not you."

"Neither do you." Brit's voice was a croaking whisper, and her eyelids fluttered.

A chuckle of relief bubbled up in Kirby's throat, but she swallowed it.

"You're not supposed to be talking," Gwydion said to Brit.

Brit flipped him off.

This time Kirby's snort escaped.

"Out." Gwydion pointed at the door. "So I can fill the patient in, and so she stops talking."

"Don't take that conversation somewhere else." Brit's voice was already a hair stronger. "If you're going to talk about me, do it in front of my face."

"Hush, or I'll gag you," Gwydion warned.

Kirby shook her head. "No he won't. He's not the sadist.'

Brit's eyes grew wide.

Gwydion pointed a finger at her and glared at Kirby.

Kirby held up her hands in surrender. "We're going. So Brit stops talking. We'll save the shit about her until she can hear us—cross my heart." That ought to be an interesting conversation.

She left with Starkad, her conflict raging stronger than before, now that Brit was conscious. She couldn't trust Brit, but was relieved she was alive. What happened in the warehouse—Brit's actions before and during—felt different than the other times. That didn't mean anything had changed. Kirby never saw the first betrayal coming, either.

But they couldn't keep Brit captive for eternity. Where was Kirby's *shoot first, self-preservation above all else* instinct when it came to Brit? It was more than self-destructive tendencies that kept Kirby from eliminating this threat. The thought of Brit being gone curdled her gut and clenched like a fist around her lungs.

And it was going to get Kirby killed.

CHAPTER TEN

Brit hadn't expected to wake up. Especially not in a hospital room, with people taking care of her. And she hated that her heart insisted Kirby was watching her with any concern at all.

After the others left, Gwydion explained what had happened.

Shot in the back of the head by one of her own. *No.* She hadn't been part of TOM for a long time, and the reflex of thinking otherwise needed to go away. There was one piece of good news buried in the middle of his story—she was pretty solidly unkillable.

And Min had saved her. She'd been brought back here, part of the team, rather than abandoned. Would Mark have done that for her? No. She doubted most of her former classmates would have, either.

Brit slept a while longer, and woke up to find Gwydion sitting by her bed, keeping watch. It might be sweet if she thought he was anything other than a captor.

She coughed, both to test her vocal cords and to draw his attention. When he turned to her, she pointed to her throat and lips. Was she okay to talk?

"Stand by." Gwydion spent the next few minutes shining a light down her throat and listening to her breath. He stepped back. "It's still a little raw, but most of the way to healed. You can talk if you don't go overboard. Give screaming a couple more hours."

"I don't have any plans for that." Brit tested the words cautiously. Everything felt fine. Apparently, she could survive a shot to the head. Or real close. "Are you my jailer for the day?" She kept her question light. He didn't deserve aggression.

"I'm your *doctor* for the day."

Kinder than any TOM physician she ever had. Her head was clear. "You didn't drug me."

"I gave you enough to keep you asleep while you were critical. Min said you preferred to avoid drugs."

They'd respected her wishes by default. The idea was foreign, even after six months of living with Min. "Thank you." It was nice to be treated like a person, rather than a commodity. She was catching hints of that kindness from Kirby, but they vanished quickly every time. "When can I be released?"

"You can get up and walk around whenever you want." He side-stepped the word *released* with ease, and gestured to a pile at the foot of the bed. "Clean clothes. You can go back to your room."

"Accompanied, I assume." At least her situation hadn't changed *too* much while she slept. The bitter thought gnawed at her.

"I assume the same, but you'll have a hard time finding better company than me." His lighthearted arrogance almost made her smile.

She wasn't ready to return to her cell quite yet. The things she'd heard in the warehouse were colliding with the encounter at the potential's home. "I need to talk to everyone. Can I make that request through you, or does it have to go to committee?" It wasn't so easy to force the teasing into her voice this time.

"If you want to dress, I'll find out what everyone else is up to." He laughed dryly. "Kidding. The only thing any of us is doing is trying to figure out next steps."

"I can help with that. You're leaving me alone?"

"Wards are in place. That hasn't changed." Gwydion almost sounded apologetic.

"I get it." She wished she didn't. The situation was wearing on her. Yes, it was her fault, but that didn't make it any less tiresome.

Brit dressed in the TOM standard uniform of jeans and a plain white T-shirt. Min had offered to buy her other clothing, but she'd worn so little of what she wanted in her life that she didn't know what to ask for. Anything besides the basics felt like a costume.

She sat on the edge of the bed, tapping a beat on her thigh, until Gwydion returned.

He gestured for her to follow, and led her down a series of hallways that shifted from sterile and white to warm and friendly.

"Aren't you worried about me memorizing the layout here?" Brit asked. "You don't want to blindfold me or something?" Min didn't, when they arrived, but she'd also been kept to a single section of the palace.

Gwydion glanced at her. "No, and not really."

"You're not that stupid." She could have phrased that more kindly, but the desire for political correctness evaporated months ago.

A corner of his mouth tugged up. "And neither are you. Walking from the infirmary to the kitchen isn't going to tell you anymore than you could figure out on your own."

"Kitchen?" Her stomach growled at the thought of food.

"Yup." Gwydion led her around a corner. The kitchen was larger than a private one, but nothing compared to the cafeteria on TOM's campus, with woodblock countertops, a six-burner stove, and two large fridges side by side.

A large rectangle table was on the opposite side of the room. Kirby, Min, and Starkad were already seated, ceramic mugs and empty plates in front of them.

"Grab a seat." Gwydion gestured.

She picked a spot at the end of the table that left a chair between her and Min. The scent of spices lingered in the air—onion, garlic, pepper, and something with a little more heat—but it was all ambient. Not like anything had been cooked recently.

Her stomach growled again. Big injuries always took a lot out of her, and this might have been the worst she'd suffered since Hel killed her.

"You wanted to talk?" Starkad was as stone cold as always.

Nice to see some things were exactly as she expected.

"She just regrew parts of her brain and throat. Let her replenish a little." Gwydion set a sandwich on a plate in front of her.

Thick sliced bread. Fresh cuts of turkey with stuffing and candied cranberries. Brit glanced at Kirby, the only person who knew she liked this.

Kirby shrugged. "The cook was told this used to be your favorite."

"It still is." Brit took a giant bite, not caring that some of the toppings dribbled out the back of the bread. These people couldn't think much less of her, and she was fucking starved.

Besides, Gwydion's request to let her eat wouldn't matter. Starkad didn't care about her comfort, beyond what she needed to be useful to him.

She crammed another bite into her mouth and washed it down with water. It was a really good sandwich.

When she'd shoved enough food in her face to keep her stomach quiet, she set the food aside. "Kirby was right. We can't wait this out any longer."

"You heard that." Kirby didn't sound surprised. "What do you mean *we*?"

Brit was part of this team, whether they liked it or not. She'd taken bullets for these people. "Who do you know on the inside?"

"You." Starkad bit the word off. "*You're* my person on the inside."

"You were there for how many decades, and you didn't make any friends?" Brit let snideness slip into her words.

Starkad's growl was primal. That was borderline terrifying. Not that she'd tell him that. "Almost a thousand years running into immortal assholes and their servants, and the list of those I trust is pretty short," he said. "Whom do you know?"

"As if you'd use any name I gave you." Brit was going back to her cell if this was an indicator of how this conversation was going to go. "*I* wouldn't even rely on those people. We were the top team. Anyone who called us *friend* wanted my position or Mark's." Except Kirby. Not that she'd ever needed to covet a top spot.

"We're getting ahead of ourselves. Why now?" Min asked.

Fair question. Would they believe Brit's answer? "In the warehouse, the soldier I shot, wasn't surprised to see me alive. He said, *The faithful will return.* And the other one said, *For Death*, before he shot me."

"Hel was a goddess of death. I don't see what's so unusual about TOM killing in her name." Min's tone was kind, but the interruption was irritating.

"*For Death* isn't Hel's thing," Kirby countered. "That's not something we were taught."

Gwydion shrugged. "Maybe it was just that one guy's thing."

98

"I think it's part of the ritual." Brit raised her voice, to speak over everyone else. "I did *a lot* of reading on that campus; most of it about how gods are killed. They don't come back, but a sacrifice in their name is powerful. You can't deny that."

"We covered this two seconds ago. That's not how Hel referred to herself." And there was Starkad's input.

Brit didn't expect this to go easily, but she'd hoped for a little bit of give. "Are you going to ignore possibilities because they came from me?"

Starkad said, "We might," at the same time Min said *no*.

"We've all been searching for months for answers about how Hel may return. This is something we haven't encountered before now, and if there's even a possibility it means something…" *Please, someone, draw a reasonable conclusion from this besides me.*

Kirby stood. Not that she needed to, in order to have all eyes on her. "We need a way to work with someone inside, who's high enough up on the ladder they have access to high-ranking information. If there's anyone left like that who isn't a fanatic, we don't have any way of knowing. This is the same thing that's stalled us for months—we don't have a way in. Has that changed?"

Silence fell over the room. That probably didn't happen very often. Brit could go into TOM, but there was no way they'd trust her to be a double agent. It didn't matter how sincere she was about not betraying them again.

"No one at TOM knows Brit is still alive, do they? We've kept her hidden…" Bless Min.

Starkad's laugh was expected.

Kirby's hurt a little more. "Yeah… no."

"I may have a way to send you in." Min focused on Kirby. Even seated, he commanded as much attention as she did.

"How?" Starkad asked.

Gwydion slammed his palms into the table hard enough to startle. "Nope. No. Hell no. Hell *the fuck* no. She's not walking back into a situation that almost killed her."

A new flavor of envy tickled Brit's tongue. What would it be like, to have someone so dedicated to her well-being?

"We have to hear Min out." Doubt sneaked into Starkad's voice.

Kirby stared at her fingernails, picking at the edges. "Do we?" Her voice was barely a whisper.

Gwydion grabbed her arm and tried to tug her toward him. She pulled away.

"This is the kind of thing you need to be in for more than one-hundred percent." Min looked between Kirby and Brit. "Both of you."

Intriguing…

"Then I suppose we'd better listen." As Kirby scrubbed her face, her hands distorted her sigh. "How do I get onto campus, and what does it have to do with her?"

Her? Hello, disdain.

Min closed his eyes and took a deep breath. When he opened them again, he stared at the table. "*Ka.* It's the spiritual doppelganger of a person, and it only emerges once they die. It can be bestowed on an object or another person, to keep the original individual's life and visage alive."

Pieces were appearing in Brit's mind, but she couldn't make them quite fit.

"'S'plain, please?" Kirby asked.

"Brit has died. Her *ka* has been released. I can give that to Kirby. She can become Brit and return to campus, and I can become the gunman who shot her."

"No." Starkad shook his head. "I gotta agree with Gwydion on this one. If you can do that to Kirby, you can do that to any of us. There's no reason to send her back in there."

"I'm sorry. Since when do you have that kind of say in how I execute my part of any mission?" Irritation crept into Kirby's voice and mingled with hesitation.

Min pushed back from the table, towering over everyone. The subtle power struggles in this conversation were fascinating, but his presence was impossible to ignore. "I don't recommend it for anyone else. Kirby and myself is already pushing limits, but it's the best chance we have. This isn't just assuming a body; it will give Kirby a copy of *all* of Brit. Her memories. Her emotions. Kirby's dealt with multiple memories before, and I've done this as well. If you haven't had someone else's life shoved into your brain, while you're infiltrating a campus full of trained killers isn't the time to start. There will be *no* more secrets. Which is why Brit has to agree as well."

Well… fuck. Everyone had secrets. Most of Brit's biggest dealt with her own insecurities. Kirby. What she hated about her life. "Show of hands. How many people here would willingly let someone—an ex-lover of all people—live in their heads?"

"I'm only barely accepting the other dozen lives I've lived. And they were mine," Kirby said.

Min sank back into his seat. "That's not a definite *yes* from either of you. We'll find another option."

Brit caught Kirby's gaze and held it. So this was what it felt like when the room collectively held its breath. It was beyond terrifying. So much more than hiding from a few pissed-off gods. Overwhelming, compared to planning to betray Hel.

"We need the room." Kirby never stopped staring at Brit. She pointed a finger at Starkad. "It's not a request."

He kissed the tip of said finger. "Hurt her if she tries anything."

"She just recovered from the last injury," Kirby said. "Go."

All three men left the kitchen. *That* was power—another kind Brit would never wield.

Kirby finally sat again, and the energy seemed to drain from her limbs. It would be a mistake to assume she'd let her guard down, but she looked exhausted. "How are you feeling?"

"Like I was shot in the back of the head?" Would this be similar to Starkad's interrogation earlier? "Except, that's not true. My throat's a little scratchy, but I'm combat ready."

"I'm glad. But I'm wondering about *you*."

What? "I'm fine." The lie came out sounding like one, and Brit winced.

"You're allowed to say if you're not feeling all right. No one here expects you to think this is an ideal arrangement. You're being held captive, regardless of the amenities, and even though you can't die, you have no idea if you'll be let go in the future. Today, for the first time, you faced off against the people you were raised with."

The events of the warehouse flashed in Brit's mind. That split second of hesitation, when a soldier recognized her. When she recognized him. The memories of training together. The competition. The camaraderie. The instinct that squeezed her finger down on the trigger regardless.

"Second time," she said.

"Right. At Kyle's house." Sympathy flashed across Kirby's face, before her mask slid back into place. She excelled at so many things, but hiding her emotions had never been a top-notch skill.

Brit would have preferred if it were. If she didn't know Kirby felt anything beyond disdain for her.

More silence. More staring. Kirby would talk soon, to clear the air. Unknowingly pulling Brit out of reliving that instant in the warehouse, over and over. Where she looked someone she'd trained with in the eye, and put a bullet in his head.

But the silence sank into Brit's bones, leaving headspace for the echo of bullets biting into concrete. The taste of gunpowder in the air. The grunts and *thunks* as bodies hit the floor.

"How do you do it?" Brit had to speak, to keep from picturing the mission. "You've killed—what?—more than a dozen of us. *Them*. And you kept going after each one." Brit had killed over and over, but she'd never looked one of her own in the eye and pulled the trigger before.

Kirby frowned and chewed her bottom lip. "It's only been eight. I tried doing it from a distance. The first team I went after, I set up like you and I used to. But sniping them felt wrong. Like I was still trapped in their training. I couldn't do it a second time. I couldn't execute them from a distance."

She blew a puff of air up, knocking aside a loose strand of hair on her face. "Maybe it was the Valkyrie in me, already shining through, or maybe I'm just a different kind of fucked up. I had to look them in the eye. I owed them that respect. The chance to face their attacker. An opportunity to change their minds."

That almost made sense. Leave it to Kirby to make face-to-face execution sound noble.

"You know they're not going to. Change their minds, that is," Brit said. "That breaks our training."

Kirby's smile was sad. "You and I did."

"After I helped them take everything from us." Brit had never admitted that out loud before. That she realized how much of the blame lay with her. She'd alluded to it with Min, but pushing the words past her lips was almost freeing.

"I know most of the teams would never take that offer. More of the soldiers might. Campus police. The students who are still enduring the suffering and indoctrination. And even if every single one I encounter spits in my face, I owe them that. They were my brothers and sisters. Those who are committed can't be allowed to live. Not with what they've been molded into. There are days I question if I should be allowed to.

"But they deserve to know why they're dying. And the ones who want out should have that opportunity as well. Which is why we have to find a way back onto campus."

Brit agreed. She believed in so little anymore, but if there was an opportunity to save even one other person from what she or Kirby went through, it was worth it. "Does it ever get easier? Killing them?"

"You tell me. How many potentials have you taken out?"

More than she could ever atone for. So many lives gone, at the whim of the gods. "I've lost count."

"No you haven't."

Brit didn't have a counter to that. The number was as etched in her mind as it had been in the barrel of her AUG. Fitting that she lost the gun the same day she took her last shot on TOM's behalf. "This is our best chance, isn't it? To save as many people on that campus as we can."

"I don't know how else we're going to get in there. We don't have the years it will take to find that one person who's like us. Who wants out. Who's not going to lie about it, one way or the other. And those kids... They were lied to. Promised a glory they'll never have. Tortured to mold them." Kirby's voice faded and the creases in her forehead deepened.

"Some people thrived. Mark."

105

"That wasn't thriving. He was as fucked up as the rest of us. He just addressed it differently."

This wasn't an easy decision. "If we do this, I'm letting you live in my head. Or letting me live in yours." The idea was terrifying, but with a hint of hope. Kirby would see Brit was sincere. Unless Kirby still didn't interpret any of Brit's thoughts as genuine.

Then there were the thoughts that were old but still existed. The bitterness. The resentment. The desperate longing. If those were in Kirby's head, would she see that they'd faded, or would Brit's everything be fresh and new?

"I've always wondered..." Kirby sighed. "I've always wondered why you did what you did. How much of what you say now is real. If any of it ever was."

The love was always real. The words screamed in Brit's mind. She'd said them so many times already, they wouldn't carry impact. Especially not today.

"This isn't how I wanted to find out," Kirby said.

But they were out of options. It didn't matter how they wished things would go. What an ideal scenario looked like. These were the cards they had, and holding them too long would get more people killed. "If you agree, I'll agree."

"You don't want to be the bigger person and sign on first?"

Brit laughed. "When have I ever been the bigger person? I'm about to let you climb into my brain."

"And I'm about to walk into a place run by gods who have looked to kill me since before I was born."

Kirby rarely looked vulnerable. The entire time they were in school, when they went on missions, even in bed, she always carried herself with a kind of impervious strength. But right now, if Brit squinted hard enough, she might see every little chink in Kirby's armor.

They really had both changed in the last few years.

Brit pushed back from the table, walked to where Kirby sat, bent at the waist, and brushed her lips over Kirby's.

Kirby pulled away. Was Brit about to get slapped? Kirby rested a finger under Brit's chin, turned her head a fraction, and kissed her on the cheek.

It wasn't what Brit hoped for, but it was far more tender than she expected, and it hummed under her skin and in her heart. She returned to her seat. "I'm in."

"Me too."

CHAPTER ELEVEN

Kirby wasn't roaming the halls tonight, and Starkad and Gwydion weren't in random parts of the castle, doing research. Both men were in their temporary room with her, shooting her frequent, worried glances.

She didn't want their concerned looks. Not because they were unappreciated, but because the entire situation sank into her bones, reminding her of what she was about to do—go back to the one place she swore she'd never return to. As the one person she'd once upon a time sworn she'd never forgive.

She sat on the bed between the men, pretending she was watching the TV. She didn't even know what was playing. An old *Planet of the Apes* movie. Or a new *Conan* one. Or something about being on Mars?

"I don't want you going back in there," Gwydion said.

It was a relief to hear him say so. A few hours ago, when she and Brit announced their decision, everyone agreed this was the right route to take. It wasn't enthusiastic, but consensus was there.

"Why are you agreeing?" she asked.

"Because I know why you're doing it. Because it's not my decision. Because I'd never expect anything less than all-in from you."

"I'd rather be going in your place." Starkad gently squeezed her thigh.

Kirby couldn't imagine. Not under these circumstances. "You really want Brit's thoughts in your head?"

"Maybe in Min's place, watching your back." Starkad's laugh was strained.

Kirby leaned forward, crossing her legs and resting her arms on her thighs. "Me too."

Min wouldn't hurt or betray her; she wasn't concerned about that. But this was a war zone, and she didn't trust anyone more than Starkad in dangerous situations.

"You're struggling with this." Gwydion moved to kneel in front of her, and met her gaze.

What Kirby intended to be a laugh came out as more of a strangled sob. *Struggling.* Understatement of the decade. Life on campus had been hard. Not the military training—she wouldn't have wanted that to be easy—but *life.* The cliques. The competition. Mark. *Brit.*

"I'm scared shitless." She didn't mean to be quite so honest. "There are days I barely believe who I am, and only some of that has to do with my past lives. The rest of my doubt comes from *there.* And now I'm going back. Pretending to be someone I'm not. Like that wasn't hard enough the first time around." She hugged herself to stop the shiver that wanted to race through her, but there was no suppressing the reaction.

Starkad pressed into her back, wrapping his arms around her and squeezing tight. The gesture wasn't a solution, but it helped hold her together. "Min wouldn't offer this if he thought there was any chance—"

"You can still change your mind," Gwydion said.

She could, but she wouldn't. Had it really only been a few months since she thought fear was delicious? A delicacy to gorge herself on? "I trust Min when it comes to this. But I can't..." If she followed this path, she'd have to acknowledge the swirl of thoughts in her head. Give them names. Recognition. "What if I get caught? What if I get people killed? What if I come back and you're not here?" The last one scared her the most. Rationally it wasn't a possibility, but she was terrified that—

This was the only time since her first life that she'd lived long enough to truly enjoy her time with Starkad. If she didn't come back from this, would the connection she had with him and Gwydion be the same in her next life? Would she lose any chance of figuring things out with Min? What if she didn't come back at all? No more lives. No more chances.

Once upon a time, that would have been a comforting thought, but now...

"Hey." Gwydion cupped her cheek, drawing her back to the *now*. His touch was comforting. Grounding. "We'll be here. Always. That never changes. It never will."

He stood, tugged her to her feet, and cradled her face. The soft brush of his mouth over hers was more of a suggestion than a reality, and it drew a gasp from her. He leaned in for another kiss, claiming her lips and pouring his soul into the connection. Into every nibble and touch and caress of her tongue with his.

There was no comparing sex with Gwydion to sex with Starkad, beyond saying they were both *amazing*. They were dramatically different lovers, and being caught between them was the ultimate experience in spicy-sweet.

So when Starkad dug his fingers into her hips, she groaned with anticipation. He pressed into her back, gripping her with a ravenous possession that both bruised and enticed. He dragged his teeth along her shoulder, and she felt the sharp point of a canine.

There were some hard rules, when it came to the pain he inflicted. The biggest one was *no knife play*. Kirby sometimes still felt the tug of wanting to cut, and Gwydion insisted on no blades in the bedroom.

Starkad had enough control over his transformation to only summon the bite, and he toed the line of that rule. His bite pierced her skin, sending a sharp sting of pleasure jolting over her, and licked the tiny wound clean, making her shiver. The connection that flowed between him and Kirby when he did that hummed through her veins and painted her world in vibrant colors.

"How lost do you want to get?" Starkad's question rolled over her.

The euphoria that came with the combination of pain and pleasure was a world Kirby could vanish into.

"As far and deep as possible?" Gwydion teased.

And there was the dick joke. As comforting and right as everything else surrounding her. She didn't want sex right now, though. "I want to stay here. I'm about to lose myself for who knows how long. Tonight, hold me. Keep me grounded."

Starkad pressed his lips softly to the back of her neck and wrapped his arms around her waist. "Of course."

She sank back into him, still holding onto Gwydion. They kept the shadows and doubt at bay but didn't completely erase her fear for what she was about to do.

CHAPTER TWELVE

The effects of a night of cuddling evaporated when Kirby came face to face with Min and Brit in the morning. Not because of who they were, but because of what came next.

The five of them were back in the kitchen, but Kirby was too wound up to eat anything.

Judging by the untouched coffee, fruit, and pancakes that sat on everyone else's plates, she wasn't the only one.

"Do you really need me here for this?" Brit asked. She'd nibbled on a strawberry, and that was it.

"You don't want to hear the rest of the plan?" Kirby didn't believe it.

"I'll stick around for that part, but I don't want... You'll see, I'm sure, once I'm in your head. Or is it the other way around?"

Even Starkad wasn't hiding his concern. "Kirby will change first. Brit hasn't had any interaction with the grunt—"

"*Erek*," Brit corrected him.

"—since before the fight with Hel, so talking to him here may give her information she shouldn't have. But he needs to be the first back to campus, and *we* want anything he can tell us. So once Kirby is Brit"—Starkad shook his head—"she'll tell Aeval where she wants to hang out for the next week or so, until it's time for her to hop a plane back east."

"We only get one attempt with these lives," Min said. "We're taking on their bodies, their minds, everything about them, but if they die, we become ourselves again." He frowned, his *fuck* barely audible.

Gwydion dropped his spoon, and the clatter made them jump. "No. Wrong. We're not doing this if there's a *fuck* element."

"Brit's *ka* has an unknown variable." The frown that settled on Min's face was concerning. "In that she can't die, but she did at one point, or this wouldn't be possible. There's a slight possibility that if Kirby were to be injured the way Brit was the other day—rendered comatose even—she'd be stuck."

That was a pretty big *well fuck*, but Kirby couldn't back down now. This was the only shot they'd had in months, and they probably wouldn't get another before it was too late. "If we're not killed, how do we turn back when it's all over? Can't you give me a safe word or something? Both of us, that we can use on the other if needed?"

"Yes." The creases in Min's forehead lessened but didn't vanish. "*Ástvinur.*"

Beloved. The word in her original language was so beautiful rolling off his tongue.

"Anything else I need to know?" Kirby asked.

114

"You can release the *ka* yourself, by focusing, but I'll be here to help when you're done, regardless. Don't fight this. If there are things about Brit that are contrary to you, your instinct is going to be to override them. Don't. The two of you will be living separate lives. She won't have access to what you do as her, unless you tell her after."

Brit pushed back from the table. "Right. I'm going back to my room." She rested a hand on Kirby's shoulder. "Good luck. And I'm sorry."

Kirby squeezed her hand, but a response didn't come.

As Brit walked out of the kitchen, Min prompted Kirby to stand, and they stepped back a few feet from the table.

"Your entire body is about to adjust itself," Min explained. "It will be more comfortable if you're upright. When I say *don't fight her*, I mean everywhere. You've got a different center of gravity. You're taller. You move differently. Brit knows how to work Brit's body. Let her."

His phrasing drove home how odd this situation was.

Kirby nodded. "I get it, in theory." And if she struggled with it in application, she had a week to adapt. Was this the kind of scenario where being a fast learner mattered? "I'm ready." She wasn't really, but she never would be. Now or never.

When Min brushed his thumb along her cheek, a light jolt raced through her, like the faintest hum of electricity.

She expected an onslaught of memories to knock her back, the way it had when she remembered her past lives. Maybe he hadn't started yet.

Her joints felt wrong. As if she was being compressed from all sides at once, wrapped in a tight cocoon. Her muscles twitched, and her legs wobbled under her. She steadied herself and focused on the floor, to ignore the spinning in her head. The tile should be farther away. Not much, but the five or six centimeters were enough to disorient her.

Her shirt was too tight in the chest. Her yoga pants stretched tightly across her hips, but were looser in the waist, and the hems met the floor.

Because I'm wearing Kirby's clothes.

She *was* Kirby.

"You're done." Min's voice sent flutters of comfort and security dancing over her skin. That was new. She was used to desire and confusion, mixed with a smattering of fear for how she reacted to him.

"How do I look?" Her voice wasn't right. It wasn't Brit's. but it was. It was the way Brit heard her own voice.

"Exactly the way you should," Min said.

That was… good? She turned to face Starkad and Min, trying to let instinct drive her movements. She stumbled. Turning around. What the fuck?

Min settled a hand on her shoulder. "Don't think about walking or any movement, any more than you normally do."

Easier said than done. An image splashed in her mind. A memory from when she was younger. Fourteen? Fifteen?

"I'm never going to get this." Frustration filled Brit, as she flopped on the practice mat. Kirby made it look so easy.

Kirby offered her a hand. When Brit accepted, the tingle of desire raced both ways. Kirby wanted to see Brit get this. To celebrate with her. To protect her until she figured things out. To find a quiet corner of campus and see what her lips tasted like.

Brit wanted the kiss. Desperately. She also wanted to be better at anything *than Kirby was. To finally land that kick. Make that impressive pin to the mat. Get a higher score in shooting. To prove to Kirby they were equals.*

"You're thinking about it too much," Kirby said. "You already know the moves. Stop listing them in your head, and just let your body react."

Brit both appreciated and hated the smug advice. She did *know all of this. "Easier said than done. You might as well tell me not to think about an elephant."*

Kirby shook the past aside, but the emotions from both perspectives lingered. "That's disorienting," she muttered.

She focused on Starkad, who watched her with an unreadable expression. Except she knew this one, because the same feelings bounced though Brit. Envy. Intensely passionate jealousy, for the way Kirby felt about him. Disdain, that he'd done so much wrong and still got to be by her side.

But Kirby didn't feel that way. Starkad had been with her since the beginning of time—her time, anyway. He was her berserker. Her savior.

Her captor. Her tormentor. Her rival.

No. Her lover. Her grace.

She pressed a palm to her forehead, wobbling on her feet.

"Stop fighting it." Min was kind. "You're not Kirby right now; you're Brit."

And apparently Brit had a lot of very specific feelings about the men in Kirby's life. "I can still hear myself. I don't want to lose me in her."

"It doesn't work that way. Kirby is still always there underneath, and you don't have to stop being you. But you do have to stop fighting Brit," Min said.

Except Kirby wanted another *goodbye* kiss from Starkad and Gwydion, and Brit wanted to get back to her room, put on clothes that fit, and get to her hideaway on the Cayman Islands. She had property there. A different identity. Money—not a lot, but enough to cover expenses for six or so months while she looked for alternatives.

Min nudged her. "This is going to be easier if you go someplace where Brit has memories and Kirby doesn't. At least until you adapt. Aeval is waiting with your things."

Kirby's feet wanted to carry her back to the breakfast table. She had to lean into this new half of her instead. She gave Starkad and Gwydion one last glance. "I'm sorry."

She let the part of her that was Brit lead her out of the kitchen and down the hall, to the room where her new things were being kept. She changed quickly. Each glance in the full-length mirror on the back of the door filled her with ambivalence.

Kirby saw the woman she had loved, who'd betrayed her over and over, but whom she kept giving another chance. Brit saw herself, and she hated having to look herself in the eye. All of her lies and inadequacies reflected back at her. The flaws she hid from everyone else, but that someone else would discover sooner or later.

That explained why Brit didn't want to stick around to see a copy of herself. This was going to be an interesting few weeks.

*

Min wished there had been a better way to give Kirby an idea of what she was heading into. The last few months with Brit had shown him hints of several insecurities. Kirby could handle the situation, but it had to be a lot to face.

Starkad looked annoyed with the way she'd left the room. "If I thought you were vengeful, I'd wonder if this was payback for my insisting Kirby be kept on the TOM campus in the first place."

Gwydion sighed. "Un-fucking-believable. Of course that's the first thing you say."

It was nice to see some things hadn't changed. The antagonism between these two, for instance. "This is harder on her than it is on you," Min said.

Starkad's scowl eased. "I know."

"But vengeance..." Gwydion drew out the thought. "Don't think you're off the hook there. I've got ideas."

"She'll be all right." Starkad almost sounded like he believed it.

Gwydion shook his head. "Keep telling yourself that."

Hadn't changed at all. When Min had seen the two of them laughing and joking, he assumed they'd put aside their animosity. He shouldn't have been fooled. "Have you two been like this for six months?"

"Like what?" Gwydion adopted an angelic expression that wouldn't fool anyone who knew him.

Starkad looked like a petulant child. "No."

The temporary truce had been because Kirby was here. Safe. In their grasp.

Min remembered that false sense of security. He'd fallen into the same delusion in her last life. He could watch Starkad and Gwydion bicker all day, or he could get on with his own transformation. "You'll want information from me once I've changed?"

"I assume, from what you told Kirby, that you'll have enough control to provide it." Starkad was issuing a challenge. This was as much a question of Min's honesty with Kirby, as it was about what he'd be able to tell them.

"I will." Min didn't lie to her. The idea was abhorrent. "I'm practiced at accessing two souls, so I won't have the struggle you saw in her. In a few days, she won't have issues with it either."

Starkad pushed back from the table, and rested a hand on the pistol holstered on his hip. "Let's do this."

Min closed his eyes and turned his thoughts inward. He evicted the outside world to drift along the thread of magic that tied him to so many other lives and souls. A vibrant cord guided him toward the last person he'd seen die, and he followed the line.

He tugged the *ka* into himself, letting it flow into his heart and mind. His arms. Fingers. Legs and toes. His body shifted with the change.

Erek. The soldier's name—his new name—was *Erek.*

Min didn't pull too hard at the memories. They'd flow as they were needed. As questions were asked or familiar environments and people were encountered.

He opened his eyes again, to see Starkad had a gun leveled at his head.

"Reassure me you're still in there." Starkad's tone was hard.

Erek laughed mentally. This was a light version of the treatment waiting for him when he returned to campus. Starkad had most likely helped implement those procedures.

"Would you prefer poetry, or a retelling of the first time I met Kirby?" Min asked in an unfamiliar voice. Erek latched onto the vividly erotic memories, and his body reacted.

Starkad lowered the firearm but kept his finger on the trigger. Min wouldn't have noticed. It made Erek wish he had a weapon of his own, though. He'd never trained with the school's old combat instructor, but based on the stories he'd heard, he was pretty sure Starkad would kick his ass.

That was one of the few things Min and Erek would probably agree on. This was a hostile mind to be sharing, full of paranoia, lust, and a desire to control or harm at any cost.

And it was Min's home for the foreseeable future.

CHAPTER THIRTEEN

Min-as-Private-First-Class-Erek stepped through a portal Aeval created, directly in front of the gates at *The Order of Mistletoe Academy and Boarding School*. He'd never seen the manicured green landscape with trees just turning for autumn, but thanks to becoming Erek, he knew where everything was.

Kirby and Brit had briefed him on what to expect next, and Erek's memories agreed, though without quite as many details.

"On the ground now, or you will *be fired upon."* The command roared over an unseen loudspeaker. Min let Erek's memory take over, as he lay on his stomach, hands behind his head. Visitors weren't greeted this way, but he was the sole survivor in a failed raid, he'd been gone for two days, and he'd just stepped through another immortal's gate.

Tension coiled through him, as he watched two pairs of boots approach.

A boot rested against the small of his back. She unsnapped his holster and removed his firearm.

An Urd cleanup team had cleared all the bodies from the warehouse after the rescue of Aeval's people. Min had to call in a lot of favors, to get assistance with an unauthorized mission, but it meant he had access to Erek's clothing and weapons, which he wore now.

"Name and rank," a woman barked.

He recognized that voice—Erek did. "Private First Class Erek." TOM soldiers didn't have last names. Hel believed the act separated them from their pasts.

"Date of birth." She was Amy, and she'd been Erek's first crush.

Erek's birthdate rolled off Min's tongue as if it were his own.

"First place you fucked me?"

Fraternizing between cadets was against the rules, though Kirby and Brit were only one example that it happened anyway. As desperately as Erek wanted it at the time, he hadn't broken that rule with Amy. "My fucking imagination. First time. Last time. Every time."

The owner of the other boots snickered.

"What happened when you tried?"

"You—" Erek didn't want to answer, though the words were right on the tip of Min's tongue. No one knew this, and now everyone was about to.

"Private." Her voice took on a dangerous edge.

If he didn't answer, they'd shoot him here, Erek's *ka* would fade, and Min would be exposed. "Library. Second floor. Study room." She'd been sitting on the table, and Erek forced his way between her legs. She'd kicked him back into a chair with her *no*. "You rested that sexy-ass boot against my nuts and told me, if I ever did that again, you'd practice your garrote skills on me while I slept."

That seemed to be a common occurrence here. A bunch of hyper-aggressive alpha girls and boys, shoved into dorms and training together, and told they could only screw on the school's clock? Not surprising. Still disgusting, but not surprising.

"And?" she asked.

Erek briefly wondered if being shot was better than admitting this. "I cried and begged you not to tell the staff, and swore to Vidar I'd never do it again."

Boots Two laughed out loud. "Is that true?" His voice told Min he was Jakob.

"Hand to Hel," Amy said.

Jakob stuck a hand in Min's face, and Amy removed her foot from the small of his back.

"Welcome back, man." Jakob helped Min to his feet. "Where you been?"

"Long story." Min kept his hands behind his back and let them bind him with a plastic zip tie. Next came the blindfold, and the headphones meant to block sound. Then Min was bundled into a Jeep. He didn't have to see or hear it; his memory told him.

The ride most likely lasted fifteen or twenty minutes longer than it needed to. When they stopped, he was marched to a new location, and the bindings on his wrists were cut. As he pulled the headphones off, he heard a door latch shut behind him.

"Private Erek." A new voice came over a new speaker. "Remove everything and place it in the bin in the wall."

Min yanked off the cloth bag keeping him blind. He was in a small room, only two meters wide in each direction, with stainless-steel walls and a textured tile floor with a drain in the middle. The cameras and speaker were hidden.

The only break in the wall was a meter square about chest level. He shoved the mask and headphones in there, then stripped. Erek had far less of an issue with his nudity than he did with admitting he cried after he tried to force himself on someone and she more forcibly stopped him.

When Min adopted Erek's *ka*, he'd hoped to glean the information they needed immediately. After all, Erek had been the one to proclaim *For Death*. But the private didn't know any more about Hel's resurrection than Brit did. It would happen if the steps were followed, and that meant a lot of killing.

Min finished stripping down, including removing the small ceramic knife strapped to his calf. The door on the bin slid shut.

"Face the opposite wall," the faceless voice commanded. It was slightly mechanical, filtered to be difficult to recognize.

Min did as ordered, and a new panel slid open, exposing another camera and what he knew to be an X-Ray machine. A few seconds passed.

"Turn right, forty-five degrees," the voice ordered.

He complied, and another two times, letting them grab pictures of his entire body.

"Stand at ease." The voice didn't give away any emotion.

Min set his feet shoulder-width apart and clasped his hands behind his back, never flinching that he was still nude.

They were looking for hidden weapons, but also comparing his body to the one they had on file. Everyone here had scars and healed bones. If his wounds didn't match, he wouldn't walk out of here as Erek.

Min wasn't concerned. Except for his mind and a locked-away access to his magic, he was Private First Class Erek. Kirby's transformation was just as complete.

Seconds ticked away into minutes. He let Erek twitch uncomfortably but didn't break his stance. Erek's mind knew everything he needed to do, to make this deception look like genuine nervousness, and not like he had something to hide.

Sliding into the course language, the casual lies, and the desire to smash his fist into something to relieve his tension was foreign to Min, but Erek understood it all.

The panel in the wall slid open again, and different clothes sat inside.

"Get dressed." The voice, no longer synthesized, was male. Familiar, but not someone Erek spent a lot of time with.

Min put on the *uniform*. Jeans. T-shirt. Sneakers. There was nowhere to sit in the small box, so he waited.

"Exit through the door." One of the walls slid open.

Min stepped into a slightly larger room, almost as barren, save for the metal chair bolted to the floor, its back to a second door. His every instinct told him not to get comfortable, and muscle memory insisted he bounce on the balls of his feet. None of this mindset was familiar, but he'd adopted people's *ka* enough times over the centuries that he knew how to let the other soul take over.

It was one of the hardest things to do without practice, and it was the other reason Kirby made the best stand-in for Brit—they had enough shared experiences and similar backgrounds that Kirby wouldn't be fighting most of Brit's instincts.

The door behind the chair opened, and Loki strode in. Erek was terrified of him, and Min let that show in the slightest of trembles. This was supposed to be an interrogation, disguised as casual conversation. Something friendly but slightly aggressive, designed to get him to slip and change his story. Min knew exactly how that worked. It was the same tactic Starkad had used with Brit.

It didn't matter. Min knew Erek's story from start to finish, and the only place it was made up was at the end. Loki wouldn't be asking anyone else for a different version.

"Private. Good to have you back in our ranks." Loki's tone was too bright. Too friendly.

It set Min's teeth on edge. "Thank you, sir."

"Care to tell me where you've been? We were worried about you. An entire strike team went missing, and you're the only one left." While Loki was a few centimeters shorter than Erek, his presence consumed the room.

"Uh… yeah. They were at the warehouse, like we thought. The god—Gwydion, right?—he found me bleeding out. I woke up in a hospital room. They took care of me, then dumped me here in front of the gates."

"That was nice of them."

"It was stupid. Who the fuck heals their enemies and sends them home?"

Loki smirked. "Gwydion. But you don't have any new scars, and he's a doctor, not a magical healer."

They'd anticipated this, too. And apparently everyone on campus knew about Kirby at this point. "That Valkyrie traitor was there too. Bitch actually healed my wounds." Min hated the way this language tasted, and despised this man's disdain for Kirby.

"Did you see anyone else?"

Min shook his head. "No, sir."

"Hear any other voices?"

"No, sir. The god, the Valkyrie, and the same white walls for two days."

Loki shrugged. "All right. Welcome back." He gestured to the door he'd walked through.

"Sir?" Min didn't like this.

"We'll be watching you for a while. Keep that in mind. Expect to be brought back here at a moment's notice." Loki turned and strolled from the room, leaving the door open behind him.

Min should be relieved this went so smoothly, but even without a soldier in his head, he knew it wasn't right. His only choice was to play along until he figured out what was going on, whether he liked that option or not.

CHAPTER FOURTEEN

Kirby-as-Brit stepped off the plane in LaGuardia Airport, and the memories rushed back twofold. The last time she'd been here, Brit was by her side, and they were in love. Not *Kirby thought they were in love.*

Seeing that moment from both minds at once altered her perspective. Brit loved Kirby as much as Kirby did Brit, and knowing that—having it rock in her head with as much reality as anything—squeezed Kirby's heart in a painful grip.

Back then, they'd walked through this same terminal hand in hand, joking about how grateful they were they didn't need condoms, because— *fuck*—those were expensive in gift shops.

Being Brit, living her life, wasn't like when Kirby recovered her own memories. There was no abrupt rush of the past, trying to crowd itself all into the same space at once. Brit's life was already there, hanging out casually and waiting until called upon, as if it were Kirby's.

And this airport called so loudly, it was deafening. This was coming home, over and over, after every mission—so many of those missions with Mark. Resentment, loathing, and disdain spilled from Brit's memories. Years spent faking everything, while she looked for an escape.

Kirby stowed the memories and continued her journey toward the taxi line. She didn't have much luggage. A few uniforms, toiletries—nothing that couldn't be replaced. She didn't expect to keep any of it beyond the TOM entrance.

She was arriving at campus nearly a week after Min, having spent the last few days living as Brit. Aeval had deposited her on the Cayman Islands, where Brit had IDs and a small stash of money. Not enough to survive on for long. Six months to a year if she was frugal.

Kirby had lived on the island while she waited, acclimating to having Brit's memories and personality in charge. She was used to a certain degree of self-doubt and destruction, but Brit was a heavy dose of self-loathing and regret. The feelings were peppered with every truth and lie Brit had told Kirby.

And there were a lot more truths than Kirby wanted to see. She'd had to stop prodding the memories, because some of them were so achingly raw.

She stepped to the curb, hailed a taxi, and was on her way to campus. When Brit and Mark took off from this place, more than six months ago, they'd left a car in long-term parking. It was a relief to not be picking that up. To not have him driving. To not have to make halfhearted conversation with the asshole who'd fucked her again and again—physically and life-wise.

Brit knew better than to tumble down that chasm of pain, and turned away even while Kirby teetered on the edge.

She steered her thoughts back toward the current mission. Analyzing the details from a removed position was safe.

The ride was over far sooner than she expected or wanted. She paid the driver and stepped onto the path in front of *home*.

She approached the campus's entrance. Any minute now, someone's disembodied voice would tell her to hit the ground, and she'd be grilled to prove she was Brit.

The closer she got to the entrance, the louder her pulse roared in her ears. Would they simply shoot her?

As she reached the gate, her senses were on critical alert. Campus police stepped from the guard house and approached. "Sergeant." The woman kept her hand on her firearm. "Welcome back."

"Thank you, Private Amy." Kirby recognized her, but Brit *knew* Amy. Her rank. How long she'd been here. Whom she hung out with, including Erek for several years, when they were younger.

"I need to know if you're going to comply," Amy said. "We're being watched. Please don't try anything."

Kirby dropped her bag and held her hands up in surrender. "Pistol at my hip. Another on my outside right leg. Happy to answer any questions."

"No questions, sir." Amy took her weapons.

Kirby didn't like this, and neither did Brit's knowledge. "Since when do we offer leniency to anyone, Private?"

"Following orders, sir. Please come with me."

The interrogation building was only a few hundred meters from the front gate—no reason to bring uninvited guests too far onto the grounds—but Kirby didn't expect to walk there. She was shown to a room with a single metal chair in the middle. No surprise, it was bolted to the floor. That was the only thing about this situation that felt right.

She didn't sit. No one had told her to, and she'd rather not keep her back to the door. It wasn't long before the door opened again, and Loki strolled through.

Well, *fuck.*

His warm smile and soft eyes made her gut sink. What was he up to? He closed the distance between them with long, confident strides.

She kept her hands behind her back, fingers twitching at the dagger strapped to the inside of her wrist.

When Loki cupped her cheek, shock spilled through her in quantities large enough to mute the revulsion. "Welcome home, lover." He murmured against her lips.

She flicked her knife into her hand and pressed it to the base of his throat in a single sweep. *It's a test.*

Loki stepped back several feet, his smile melting into a smirk. "You led Private Amy to believe you'd handed over all your weapons."

"And *you* should have had her frisk me and put me through the same check-in you give every person who's been MIA." This part was easy. Kirby and Brit shared an open disdain for Loki, as did a large number of campus residents. He was the public face of the campus, but Hel had been behind the inner workings. "I assume you're responsible for the stupid command to let me walk in here however I wanted?"

Loki took the single seat and crossed one ankle over the other knee. "You're our best and brightest." Sarcasm bled into his reply. "The prodigal-fucking-daughter. I want them to see you getting special treatment."

"Why?" This couldn't be good.

"You're the Chosen One, lover. Gifted by Hel herself, to return after her destruction. How'd that all go down, by the way?"

She wanted to throat-punch him every time he called her *lover*. She settled for flipping her blade in the air, catching it, and throwing a well-aimed shot at his shoulder.

Loki snagged the dagger from the air, vanished, and buried it in her arm when he reappeared next to her.

Kirby screamed at the pain that tore through her, but never paused. She grabbed the hilt and stabbed at Loki's gut.

He was already gone, back in the chair.

She recovered from the stumble and fixed a glare on him.

"You certainly fight like Brit." Loki's grin was gone. He studied her with a critical eye. "Bleed the way she should. Do you need to get that looked at?"

Kirby wiped the blade on her jeans, sheathed it, and pressed against the already-clotting wound. "I'll be fine in a few hours. Do you want answers, or are we playing games?"

"You know better than that. Games can provide more answers than questions."

Kirby hadn't missed anything about being here, and the culture of bullshit was on the top of her TOM-Sucks-Sweaty-Balls list. "How many staged attacks will it take, for you to find out what happened with Hel? Because I'll tell you right now."

"Start before then." Loki looked at ease in the way no one should when they were in the middle of an interrogation room. Then again, he was the interrogator. "Debrief me on your last mission."

Kirby let out a long sigh. "Well, you know we ran into an old friend. We thought we'd killed her. Mark wrapped a fucking garrote around her neck"— Kirby faltered at a wash of hundreds of overlapping memories, hers and Brit's—"and she was dead on the ground when we walked away." Her voice wavered. A ghost of a gunshot throbbed behind her ribs, carried on conflicting emotions. Kirby, feeling betrayal over and over. Brit, telling herself shooting Kirby was the only way to save her life, though she didn't know why.

"Something wrong, Sergeant?" Loki's tone was flat.

Brit had so much regret for what she'd been forced to do, to earn Hel's trust. Every moment her mind drifted, she fell back into shooting Kirby again and again, and hating herself, even though it hadn't been real. Even though it was all for Kirby in the end.

Kirby shook her head. It didn't rattle the past or the pain loose, but it freed her vocal cords. "Just reliving the moment. Hel tested me with what happened there. Put me through it a thousand times, if it was any. To prove my loyalty. Had me relive killing Mark. Let me finally put a bullet in Kirby's head." Brit had starkly different feelings about each person, but there was no reason to let Loki see anything except satisfaction.

"Hel must have liked what she saw," Loki said. "Do continue. With reality, not the test."

"I shot Mark. I hated the fucker, and he pushed one too many buttons, because yeah, seeing Kirby alive after all that time was a shock, and then he eliminated her. After that, I went after Starkad. Tried to kill him, too."

Loki gestured for her to go on. "And? How'd that work out for you?"

"I'm guessing you know he's immortal."

"For centuries now." Boredom was leaking into Loki's voice. "And?"

"And... did you know"—Kirby-as-Brit stalled on a truth everyone knew at this point— "Kirby's a Valkyrie? She stopped me. *Fuck*, that hurt."

"So that's when you found out. Everyone here has been told who and what the traitor is."

This was tiresome. "You obviously don't want the entire drawn-out story," Kirby said. "Short version—Starkad paid me a nice lump of cash to fuck off, and dumped me in Europe. I kept waiting for someone to come after me, and when I found Hel's *weakness*, I thought if I killed her, I'd buy myself some time. That didn't go according to plan— because of course it didn't—and I realized I'd been wrong to turn on the group that raised me. I went back to her and begged forgiveness."

"Yeah." Loki examined his nails. "Big fight that wrecks part of Wales. Hel dies. Supposedly so do you. And then you show up here, six months later, strolling in like nothing happened. Where have you been?"

"Lost. Wandering. My brain was muddled after I woke up, and I've been sorting things out. This is home, though. It always has been, it always will be. Any other questions?" Brit had always been the ultimate at hiding her feelings behind a mask. If Kirby had to be spewing this bullshit without the mental help, she'd crack. Probably try to kill Loki again.

Loki stood and straightened his suit. "Private Erek came back almost a week before you."

Her arm had stopped bleeding, and the dried mess itched. She flexed her fingers, wanting to scratch, but not wanting to reopen the wound. "Who? Oh yeah. A grunt."

"They prefer to be called *soldiers*." Loki chuckled.

"Good for them. A lot of people come and go. Do you have a list you'd like to walk through with me?"

Bored amusement vanished behind Loki's irritated snarl. "As you said, *short version*. He went missing. So did you. When our people encounter Kirby, they tend not to return. Two of you have come back within a week of each other."

She wasn't supposed to know anything about where Erek had been or the circumstances behind his release. "From what I've seen, Kirby plays fast and loose with who she fucks, and she's not as removed about it as she tells herself. Did you ask him if Valkyrie pussy feels any different than the regular kind?"

Loki blinked across the room again, reappearing nose-to-nose with Kirby. "Everyone here believes you're a sign that Hel will return. I don't know where Hel got that bullshit, because gods don't come back from destruction. Not even in Urd's world. But I'm letting you walk out of here, to feed their faith. You're being watched. Always."

"Wouldn't expect anything less." This was the point where she was supposed to quake just a little at Loki's threat. It was nice, to not have to hide that fear. She'd expected scrutiny, but not from him. Not immediately.

That needed to be her last mistake while she was here.

CHAPTER FIFTEEN

Brit's room was still available. There were a limited number of single-person apartments for the sniper teams, but more than a dozen individuals had died in the last few years, and they weren't easy to replace.

Kirby took a hint of regretful satisfaction from that.

As she strolled through the grounds, Loki-appointed grunt on her heel, memories trickled back. Kirby's and Brit's.

She stepped inside the building where the snipers lived, and the avalanche slammed into her. Of the last time Kirby was here. Being marched to the hearing by campus police, confusion and irritation melting to disbelief and ultimately devastation at the betrayal.

Brit had a few possible routes to get back to her room, but she always took the one that brought her past Kirbys old place. Kirby followed the path, letting Brit's habits drive, and struggling to sift through her thoughts.

The setting in her memory was the same, but the details were different. *Mark's smirk made her blood run cold. That was worse than the calm, neutral expression he'd been wearing. "Tomorrow morning, Kirby's going down."*

"What are you—"

"Nothing she won't recover from. Just a little disciplinary action." Mark let go of Brit. "For everything she's done to me. To you."

She hasn't done anything wrong to me. *The protest stuck in Brit's throat. Why couldn't she say something? Why couldn't she stand up for Kirby?*

Brit describing her feelings about the situation was nothing compared to living them. Fear, disgust, and bile rose in Kirby's throat, and she swallowed them back. Brit had betrayed Kirby. She knew it. She hated everything about it. She couldn't stop the heavy blanket of remorse and self-loathing that wrapped around her. Binding her thoughts and limbs. Choking her until she wobbled on her feet.

"Are you all right, sir?" His name was Richard. He'd been in some of Brit's classes when he was younger. Kirby had even trained him, but she didn't remember his name. Brit did.

His question helped ground Kirby. "I'm good. It's weird, being back. But good." She needed to get it together now. One thing Brit was infinitely better at—hiding how she really felt.

They reached her room, and she thanked Richard, then closed herself off from the world. The apartment was barren of personal effects. There was furniture. A stack of bedding sat on the mattress in the bedroom. All of Brit's stuff was gone.

Not that she'd had anything she cared about. She expected the mission when she gave her own location to Starkad to be her last here. She'd left things behind—photos, books, trinkets—but it had all been disposable.

Here in the silence, it was easy to let the past wash over her. So many feelings. She dropped onto the bed without making it, and bathed in emotion. She wasn't supposed to be here.

Never again.

Kirby had told herself that about Brit.

Brit had told herself that about Mark.

He'd fucked Brit here. So many times. She hated him for it. Hated herself for not doing more to stop him. Hated everyone around her who saw, but let him assault her anyway, because maybe Brit would suffer enough to lose her ranking.

Looking back it was easy to see she could have done something. As she relived those moments, the fear that kept her paralyzed while he pounded inside her was still a potent copper tang on her tongue.

The knock that yanked her into the *now* was a welcome relief. She didn't care who it was; it wasn't Mark.

She opened the door. "Cyclops." She used his call sign with the fakest of genuine-looking smiles. What the fuck was he doing here? He was another of the snipers. Like Brit, as inner circle as it got—one of Hel's Nobles.

Hel had encouraged them to pick names for each other. During training, this guy had had a habit of hitting the target's eye. Right eye, every time. It became his trademark shot, and the name *Cyclops* stuck fast

Kirby had never had a call sign. She led the pack, but she'd never been part of this group. Partly Hel's doing, she assumed. And probably just as much her own.

Cyclops' grin was as bright and cheery as Brit's, and likely just as insincere. "Welcome back, Kitten. We missed you."

Bullshit, they did. Brit was *Kitten* because one of the other women—Venus—had compared her to one after Brit pulled some dirty moves in a sparring match. Venus's exact words had been, *She only looks soft and fluffy. She'll tear your throat out, just like a kitten.*

"Same." Brit meant it even less than Kirby expected. The only time Nobles were nice to her was when they needed something. Typically, they were happy to look the other way while she struggled.

"I relieved Richard. Figured you might want a friendly face standing watch, your first day home," Cyclops said.

"Be careful with that. He's Loki-assigned."

Cyclops's smirk grew. "So I hear. We only let Loki think we answer to him sometimes. And we won't make a habit of this, but if you ever need some alone time, let us know." He didn't have to define *us*. He meant any member of the nobility.

"Thanks." She wished she could believe they really had her back. That would make life here easier.

He waved a casual hand. "You'd do the same for us. Rumor is you came back. alone?" As in, without her partner.

"It's true."

"I'm glad. We all are." He stepped back. "Get settled and we'll all catch up in a few days."

There wasn't much for Kirby to do, as far as *getting settled* was concerned. Her dresser and closet had been stocked with the standard uniform, a few workout outfits, and the kind of plain white panties and bras that were super sexy to someone with the right fetish.

It all fit right and didn't itch, so she wasn't complaining.

The next morning, Kirby's schedule was open. She wasn't going to be assigned to any missions or a new partner. Even if they trusted her, there was no one to pair her with who sat at her skill level. She needed to get into Hel's office again, but had to wait until she wasn't being observed twenty-four-seven.

Her options to fill her days were working out, target practice, and reading. Books called Kirby's name; she loved historical romance. Reliving those time periods of her past lives, even if they rarely got the details right.

Brit preferred older books. She'd devoured everything she found in the campus library that had to do with the gods. She even hit up the fantasy novels and comic books, looking for hints. She'd been searcing for ways to destroy the gods who made up the TOM board for a long time. Maybe she'd missed something, though. In the prophecies or somewhere.

The library would wait. Brit had a routine when she wasn't prepping for a mission, and it was time to get back to it. Coffee in her room. Copious amounts of water. Shooting range by seven thirty—after the early risers, and before classes started. Brit didn't mind putting on a show, which was what happened if she hit the range while younger students were there, but practice time was for practicing.

Kirby was good with a little more isolation. Nobility were the only people allowed to keep firearms in their rooms, but no ammo was allowed in living areas. Brit had lost her AUG on her last mission, but it would have been confiscated like everything else she returned with. She'd have to borrow a range gun.

She arrived to a blissfully empty outdoor range and checked out a Desert Eagle .40, an AUG, and two-hundred rounds for each. The scents of grass and gunpowder lingered in the air as she walked to a station. One of the few memories of this place Kirby didn't mind.

She stepped up to the farthest lane from the entrance, and settled her things in the steel booth.

Kirby ran through two magazines of ammo with the forty as a warm-up. Casual shots, to test the weapon's weight, recoil, and sights. It was definitely a range weapon, with a warn barrel that had to be aimed three degrees to the right and up five centimeters, to hit the target.

When she was comfortable with what this gun could do, she moved into speed trials. It had been too long since she timed herself. The results ought to be interesting. The exercise was simple—load two magazines, work through them in rapid fire, then reload both and repeat. The stopwatch in each lane was voice activated, so she'd call *Start* and *Stop* for each iteration.

Kirby finished the exercise once, and her time was faster than it had ever been. That wasn't possible. She had kept up with her skills, but not like this. Four more times, and each time fell in the same *Kirby's Personal Record* category.

But, of course it did. She was Brit, and Brit was a better gunman.

She was prepping to follow a similar routine with the AUG, when the range buzzer sounded to indicate someone else was entering the area. She stepped back from her booth to see an entire company of grunts streaming through the door. She should have had the field to herself for at least another half an hour. Time for Kirby to leave.

Min-as-Erek stepped into view. He was talking to and laughing with someone else. His gaze flicked over her with no recognition.

Their commander barked off spots for each of them to fall into, placing Min directly next to her. This might not be a setup, but it sure felt like one, and if looked like a duck and quacked like a duck...

Brit would stay if a random company showed up. She didn't care for the interruption, but finishing her regimen took priority.

Kirby stayed. As she got comfortable with her assault rifle, the sound of magazines clicking into place and gunshots ringing out said she wasn't the only one.

She moved on to testing her speed. She was on the routine for the fourth time, when she realized all other gunfire had stopped. The stopwatch read off her time, and a chorus of surprise rippled through her new audience.

"And *that*, privates, is why the sergeant is nobility," their commander called. "Maybe someday, with enough practice, one or two of you will be good enough to lick her boots."

Kirby mentally rolled her eyes, but beaming warmth spread through her. She moved back to make eye contact with Commander Gary. "Unlikely." Her tone was friendly. It was time to wrap this up. Sharing the field was okay. But her presence was distracting them, and she wasn't here as an exhibition piece.

Next up—stretching, a full run around campus, a shower, and finally her first meal. She took the fruit, toast, and massive pile of scrambled eggs back to her room. Another perk of being nobility.

She settled into the chair next to her desk to eat. Her muscles were tired, but energy raced through her body and mind, carried on the comfort of knowing what each next step was in her day.

Library time. The words screamed in her skull like an alarm. If she didn't go now, Mark—

Was gone. He wasn't going to be knocking on her door. Barging his way in. Insisting they hang out to *strengthen their bond as partners*. None of that would happen ever again.

The impulse to leave *now* itched in her veins, despite her knowledge. It clawed at her throat and hammered in her ears, until she couldn't focus on anything else.

"Library it is," Kirby announced to the empty room. She'd wanted to go anyway.

The campus library was filled with an amazing collection. Fiction; non-fiction; one disguised as the other to an outside observer, including mythology, prophecy, and everything else religion- and spirituality-based TOM felt was appropriate to fill the shelves.

Rows and rows of wooden bookshelves lined the main floor, as well as the five above that. Private study rooms dotted the outside walls, and long wooden tables sat near the front desk.

The third from the doorway was Brit's favorite. When she sat there, she gave off the appearance of a model soldier and student, and was always in public view. Mark had rarely approached her this way.

A knot formed in Kirby's gut, from Brit being sucked into the memories, and from herself that Brit lived it. Kirby had hated Mark and the harassment, but he'd doubled down on Brit. It only got worse when Kirby was gone.

She started in the same place Brit always did. *Religious History.* In this library, that included glorified tales of Odin, Freya, and Thor—the backstabbing, egotistical asshole. If modern fiction writers had any idea who Thor really was, they'd relegate him to a worse villain role than they put Loki in.

Kirby grabbed three heavier books that Brit had been over several times, about gods who had died in the past. Brit was convinced there was something here, but she could never find it. However, where Brit was looking for information about destroying a god, Kirby wanted to know if any had been brought back. It would take time to read through all the material, and while she was on a tight timeline, she also wasn't doing much else within it.

Odin's death was covered in great and gloriously accurate detail—not a surprise, considering where she was. He'd been a willing blood sacrifice in Thor's name, in a time of war. That wasn't the kind of thing anyone was meant to come back from; it diminished the sacrifice.

Malsumis had been sealed away by Vidar, Hel, and others. She remained trapped. A footnote said her imprisonment might have driven her brother insane, but there was nothing else about the brother.

Neit, from the same pantheon as Gwydion, had died in the Second Battle of Moytura, and remained deceased. Kirby had known him in one of her early lives. He was fanatical about war, but nice enough when there wasn't a battle raging.

Quetzalcoatl sacrificed himself with regret and shame, and never returned.

Balder was still dead, killed by mistletoe—a feat Loki was so proud of he'd named an entire organization after the plant. The Titans had never been freed from Tartarus. Prometheus was eternally bound. In fact, Loki was the only god she found in the pages who'd once been bound and was now free.

Over the next few days, Kirby easily fell into Brit's old routine. The familiarity of it was calming, even with the overlying shadow of oppression that came from being here.

She didn't find anything new in the books, though. Between Kirby's experiences in her first life, and Brit's existing knowledge, everything she consumed was old news. If she had time to read every book in this library, she might find something.

But if she didn't figure out Hel's plan soon, almost every person on this campus would die. Regardless of how Kirby felt about the place, her gut churned at the thought of that much loss of life for a god's need to live.

CHAPTER SIXTEEN

Brit recognized that Min was good company. Appreciated his kindness despite the fact that he was her jailer. Was even starting to see him as a friend.

But she didn't realize just how much she enjoyed finally having someone decent to spend time with, until he was gone.

Spending most of her time in her current room in Aeval's castle was still a better situation than so many she'd been in. She'd been given a wide roaming range. She could walk to the workout room where she'd sparred with Kirby, and to the kitchen.

Gwydion brought her books on a regular basis—she wasn't picky about content, as long as she could read something—but she went through those quickly, and he didn't tend to stick around to make conversation.

Brit was lonely. She hated the silent, gnawing pit that grew inside, devouring her, when she had to spend days at a time by herself. TOM gave her so many skills, but they stole an important one from her—she didn't know how to exist alone, with only her own thoughts for company.

The knock on her bedroom door was a relief. It would be Gwydion, and she'd appreciate the visit even if he only stayed for a few minutes.

She set aside a book she hadn't been paying attention to anyway. "Come in."

When Starkad stepped into the room, surprise jolted through her, mixed with equal parts excitement and fear. *Something to do.* He hadn't hidden his disdain in her time here, and butting heads with him was a fascinatingly frustrating challenge.

He was dressed casually, in jeans and a T-shirt one size too big, to hide a gun nestled against his back. He was going out in public, and he wanted to blend in. As much as was possible for a modern-day Viking. "You up for a mission?" he asked.

She laughed. Had he grown a sense of humor overnight?

He raised an eyebrow.

"You're serious?" She could get out of here for a little while? "Why?"

"Before he left, Min gave us everything Erek knew that had the most remote chance of being useful. We're going after a book he overheard a Noble team talking about, and you may have insight."

Of course. It was all about what she could do for him. Did she care about his motivation, if she got something positive out of it?

"And I figure even kittens need to get out sometimes." His tone was flat.

The anger and hurt that surged through her at his use of her TOM call sign caught her off guard. Why had she shared that piece of information with him? "Don't. *Never* call me that again." She forced calm through her veins, one agonizing centimeter at a time.

"Noted. The offer stands. Are you interested?"

"Yes. Absolutely."

"You don't want details?"

Brit yanked on her shoes, and twisted her hair up under a cap to hide the blond. "You'll give them to me. We'll talk as we walk." Her loneliness was already sliding away. She could lock it in the back of her mind for a while.

"Wear something baggy. I have a jacket for you," Starkad said.

In other words, Brit needed to hide who she was and would be carrying a weapon. She almost asked if he was serious a second time, but she didn't want to give him a reason to change his mind.

She joined him in the hallway. "What do I need to know?"

"A seller in Spain has the book TOM is looking for. They have buyers coming to view it tomorrow. Assumption is, it's a team. The bookseller is also a friend of Gwydion's, so we get to look at the book today. We go in, we examine it, we get out." Starkad led the way toward a part of the palace Brit hadn't seen yet.

She got to do all sorts of new things today. The cloud that had settled on her mood was lifting. "But there's a possibility it won't go smoothly."

"Always." But he thought this risk was notable.

Enough to arm her? She knew it but didn't quite believe it. Did this place have an armory? How wicked would that be—a faery palace with a room full of weapons? Non-iron weapons? An obsidian handgun hardly seemed practical, though it might be pretty. They probably had a lot of Glocks with titanium barrels and firing pins.

They rounded the next corner. *Oh.* It was the hallway leading to the conference room she'd seen when they first arrived. If this was the biggest disappointment today, she'd take it.

Gwydion was waiting in the room, a number of items on the table in front of him, including holsters, a pair of Glocks, and an oversized hoodie. He wore a suit. It might make him look tame, if it weren't for the tattoos peeking up over the collar of his shirt. Kirby would love that look. Could Brit get tattoos on an immortal body? Obviously there was a way, if Starkad and Gwydion had them, and she still scarred.

Would she do that just to catch Kirby's attention? Not *just*, but it would add weight to her decision.

Why was she even considering it? Kirby was done with her.

"Yours." Starkad pointed to the jacket and one of the holsters and guns. "If you draw on anyone who's not a threat, remember I'm faster."

Arrogant fucker. Brit looked between him and the weapons. *You're serious?* She choked back the question, checked the magazine and chamber to count rounds and make sure one was loaded, and holstered the pistol. Her shirt hung over it, and the jacket helped hide the bulk as well, but her clothing was as much to obscure her size and shape as it was to disguise a gun.

Starkad secured his at the small of his back. Not ideal, but discreet, and with his expertise, he probably had no trouble getting to it. Gwydion's would be under his suit coat.

The information ticked through her brain automatically, like any routine. It was familiar, and that was disturbingly comforting.

"When we meet the shop owner, let me do the talking." Gwydion focused as much on Starkad as he did on Brit. "Offer deference and respect."

"Be polite. Don't make waves. Act like a reasonable human being." Brit was made for blending in social situations.

Gwydion narrowed his gaze. "Deference and respect. This a dragon."

"No." Brit laughed. "Are you kidding? You're serious. A fucking dragon? Dragons are real. No shit." This was better than an armory in a faery castle.

Starkad's mouth twitched. If he wasn't careful, he might smile and crack something.

"Dead serious." Gwydion didn't hide his amusement.

Some days Brit loved knowing another world existed on top of the one most people lived in. "I'll behave. Bow. Whatever's required."

"Polite is sufficient." The spot in front of Gwydion fuzzed, as if a blurry filter had been applied to that door-sized portion of the room.

Starkad gestured to the gate back to the human plane. "Right behind you."

Brit hung back. "I'd like to know the shop layout and prepare an exit strategy. See a map, a blueprint—something."

"The shop layout is... fluid," Gwydion said. "It adapts to its owner's needs. I've never seen more than one way out, though."

Talk about fire hazard. "I don't like that," Brit said.

Starkad's frown—even deeper than normal—said he didn't either. "It is what it is. We'll adapt as needed."

Not reassuring.

Brit stepped through Gwydion's portal and to the side, letting the environment wash over her as she surveyed the landscape. They were in a narrow alley lined with old stone buildings. She'd seen enough back streets in her life that it shouldn't be remarkable, but this time was different.

The noise from the next street over, the scents of car exhaust and fresh-baked bread, and the sunshine that barely filtered in between the buildings tasted amazing. Like careless possibility. It didn't matter that she was still a prisoner and had no idea if that would last weeks or decades.

They headed toward a more populated street and blended with foot traffic. Gwydion walked behind her, and Starkad stayed close enough that his arm constantly brushed hers. Their positions and proximity were meant to look casual to any observers, and remind her she was being watched.

Brit was fine with that. If she did plan on running, this was a lousy place to do so. She didn't know the layout of the city. Didn't have resources here. Was currently safer than she ever had been with TOM.

She still had issues with the situation, but out here, the pressing loneliness evaporated.

"So, how do you know this… person?" She glanced over her shoulder at Gwydion.

"Same way anyone knows anyone. Life." Starkad's gruff tone was back.

So much for the polite reprieve. "I'm sorry. I wasn't asking you."

"No, but he'd give you an honest answer," Starkad said.

Brit rolled her eyes. Gods forbid she learn things about the people around her. "You give me an awful lot of grief for what I did to Kirby." Of course he did. Brit's sins were extensive. Now that she'd started this line of conversation, though, she didn't want to turn back.

"You're surprised?" Starkad asked.

"No. I was stupid. I was selfish and thoughtless. I own that. But I think you've got demons of your own that you're projecting on me." Where did that come from? Not that she wanted to take the words back.

Gwydion sighed. "Do you really want to antagonize and psychoanalyze a thousand-year-old wolf?"

156

No. Maybe. The sunshine and not-so-fresh air might be getting to her, but Brit wanted to needle Starkad the way he did her. Just once, she wanted to get under his skin. "You let her stay in that place. You lied to her about who you were. You watched her suffer. You broke her fucking ankle in order to—"

"To teach her a life-saving lesson."

Except it hadn't worked. Kirby never learned the *don't let anyone know how you feel about someone* lesson, and it did almost take her life. "To keep her away from me." If only it had.

Starkad growled, and the people nearest them on the sidewalk took several steps away. "If you point is that I've got sins, I know it. She knows it. They don't diminish yours."

"True." Brit wasn't deterred. "But they do make me wonder why you think you deserve that high horse you look down on me from."

Gwydion made a noise. A snort? A laugh? A cough? Nice to know he was enjoying the show.

"You won't like my answer. He sure as fuck doesn't." Starkad jerked his head in Gwydion's direction.

Brit was having too much fun poking the wolf. Maybe she should back off soon. Or not. "Does that tell you something about the nature of your justification?"

"Every decision I made, every time I kept something from her or put her in a bad situation, I thought I was doing what was best for her," Starkad said.

Brit opened her mouth.

157

"I don't know if I was or not"—Starkad shot her a dark glare—"but at the time, I thought so. That's what makes me different. Every decision you made—every betrayal—was for you. To make your life easier. To make *you* more comfortable."

This wasn't fun after all. He was right, but that didn't mean Brit liked the reminder.

"Two doors ahead. That's us." Gwydion gestured at an entrance with picture windows on either side that were filled with books. Elegant gold lettering flowed across one pane of glass, stating that the shop was *The Dragon's Hoard*.

Brit tried to summon her earlier enthusiasm, but it was buried under a fresh pile of *you brought this on yourself.* "Not the last betrayal. That was never about me." The retort didn't come out with as much force as she wanted.

"That's the only reason you're here. To Kirby, it means maybe you can be redeemed. To me, it means you gave up, and that's not enough of a reason for me to trust you." Starkad reached the shop door first and held it open.

Brit passed him to step inside. "Lucky for me, you're not the person I have to prove myself to." She should make a mental note to steer clear of that battle in the future, but now she was irritated, and Starkad was her target. She'd find a different angle for attack.

"Welcome to The Dragon's Hoard," a woman—girl?—behind the counter greeted them. She was shorter than Brit, barely five feet, and her waist-length hair was white low-lighted with black and framed a face that could be twelve or twenty-five. She wore a strappy sundress and a bright smile.

Must be nice to be so carefree. She probably didn't have any idea how true the shop's name was.

Gwydion stepped around Brit and approached the counter, his head slightly bowed. "Artura. Thank you for making time in your schedule for me." His tone was almost reverent.

"I always have time for you, *mo chara,* but you never call. Never write."

Gwydion laughed. "I suppose the centuries have gotten away from me."

Was this—? No. This understated woman was a dragon? Brit loved it.

"Who are your friends?" Artura asked.

"Starkad and Brit."

Artura came around the counter and stopped with her face centimeters from Brit's. Her eyes were a vibrant violet. "You're fascinating."

"I'm really not." Heat flooded Brit's face. Part of her had always wanted to be the person who stood out, but in her line of work, making an impression in the streets could be deadly. "It's not like I'm a dragon or anything." Was she allowed to say that? She ducked her head.

"You're far more interesting. I've meet others like me, but I've never seen anything like you. Dead but not." Artura gave a clap and looked at Gwydion. "You always bring me the best gifts. You wanted to see a book?"

That didn't sound right. "Excuse me. I'm not anyone's present." Brit didn't want to offend the magnificent-beast-in-Lolita-form, but she hadn't signed on to be handed off.

Artura's laugh was throaty and chilling, in stark contrast to everything else about her. "Quite delightful. No, dear. Meeting you is the gift."

"Oh. Same." Was that the appropriate way to respond?

"This way." Artura led them past aisles and stacks of books.

The scent, the wall-to-wall spines, and so many titles Brit had never seen before made her swallow a whimper. This place was borderline erotic. She could lose herself here for hours. Or days. If she asked nicely, would Gwydion let her stay under the watchful eye of the odd dragon lady?

Probably not, but a girl could dream.

They followed the maze of bookcases in a circle that ended with them near the front entrance again, in a round-about way. The room Artura led them to was about twenty-six meters by twenty-six meters, with a wooden table surrounded by chairs taking up about half the space. The remainder was occupied by a few more plush seats with lamps next to them. It looked like the perfect place to escape and read.

Artura snapped her fingers. A box of latex gloves appeared on the table, and a heavy book in her hands. "Be gentle with it, please. The knowledge contained in here doesn't exist in many places. As a reminder—it's promised to a different seller, and I won't budge on that. It's not about the money; it's about promises made and transfer of information."

Which was fine. If they bought the book, TOM would know they'd been here.

"Thank you," Gwydion said.

As Artura left, they all donned gloves, and Gwydion carefully opened the tome. The pages were heavy with thick ink. The book was written in English—not a contemporary dialect, but still English. Probably not an original prophecy about Hel. Maybe a retelling or a more modern interpretation.

Silence settled in the room as Gwydion turned pages, and Brit and Starkad read over his shoulder.

"This is about the Anglican Church." Brit spoke to herself as much as the men. "Hel's teachings don't tend to touch Christianity."

"That you know of." Gwydion drummed his fingers on the table, his gaze focused on the book.

"She's right," Starkad said.

Probably not the time for Brit to be smug that he'd admitted she knew something. "Hel also doesn't send people on meaningless scavenger hunts. There's something in here we're not seeing, and I don't know if we can uncover it with an hour or two of staring and nothing to cross-reference."

Gwydion pulled out his phone. "We'll photograph it. That'll be a good starting point. And hang out here for the rest of the day, seeing if there's something a copy won't show."

He turned back to the first page and snapped a photo.

This was going to take a while. Time for more needling. "Why'd you let Kirby go? Back to TOM, I mean." Brit looked at Starkad.

"Why did you?" Starkad didn't spare her a glance. "I'm honestly surprised you were willing to let her in your head."

This conversation wasn't getting turned back on Brit again. "TOM has always been in my head, so it's not like I've ever been alone with my thoughts." She hated so many of the things that lived in her mind, but. "At least now one of you will believe the things I say."

"Is that the only reason? She's your lie detector now?" Starkad raised an eyebrow but kept his gaze on what Gwydion was doing.

No. There was a chance Kirby would see the inner workings of Brit's mind and decide none of her actions had been justified. Having access to Brit's thoughts didn't mean Kirby would view them through the same lens.

"If there's anyone in this world I trust not to misuse that information, it's Kirby." Because as much as Brit sometimes hated her for how gloriously perfect she was, Kirby was genuine with her kindness. Her trust. Her heart. "And she can't hate me more than she already does."

"She can hate you more, because she's never let you die." Starkad finally gave Brit his full attention. Was that a hint of emotion in his response?

Had she struck a nerve? "You'd do the same—let her take your place if it came down to it." Wouldn't he? "Wouldn't you?"

"This conversation is over." Starkad looked at the book again.

That was telling. "I feel obligated to point out how obvious a non-answer like that is."

Starkad gripped the back of the chair he stood next to, his hands shaking and his knuckles turning pale. The faint sound of cracking wood filled the air.

Brit clamped her mouth shut. She'd scored a hit. Why wasn't there more satisfaction? She turned her attention to Gwydion's photography. The thick pages made the book look longer than it was. He was about three quarters finished.

The only sounds in the room were the scuff of gloves of paper and the creak of turning pages. This was distinctly uncomfortable.

If Brit promised to behave, could she go wander the stacks, looking for related material to this book? That seemed even more unlikely now that she'd successfully poked the wolf.

"Kirby doesn't know me anymore." Starkad's soft voice was jarring. "She has no idea what I've done over the centuries."

How bad could it be?

Brit understood the depth of that question; people were assholes. Mark. Hel. But as much as she despised and envied Starkad, some sins seemed beyond him. "You were a killing machine in her first life. Literally the gods' guard dog."

Starkad had released the poor chair, but his hands were clenched into fists. "There are worse things than taking a life on the battlefield. You know that."

"If you don't trust her with those parts of you, what are you doing in her life?" Gwydion shut the book.

Starkad made a noise that was half-barking-laugh, half-whimper. "You'd let her in your head?"

"She's already there." Sadness and certainty sang in Gwydion's response.

Brit almost choked on the sweetness of his words, and she loved sugar. The sentiment was painfully enviable. "That's disgustingly poetic."

"I'm serious," Gwydion said.

"Afternoon." A faint but familiar voice filtered into the room, and Brit's heart stopped. *Blossom.* One of Hel's Nobles. "I'm Tiff. We spoke a few times about a book you have?"

"Of course. I wasn't expecting you until tomorrow." Artura was cheerful and polite.

"We're going. *Now*," Brit whispered. She didn't care if Starkad had other feelings on the matter.

He nodded, and the three of them slipped out the door and back into the stacks. They followed a similar path to the one they'd taken in, but this planted them several meters away from the register when they emerged at the front of the shop.

Artura was just returning with the book in hand. "Would you like to look it over first?" She held up a pair of gloves.

"No. If you say it's the right one, I'll take it."

There was no one with her. Brit's pulse roared in her ears. Where was Fumbles? She shot Starkad a questioning glance.

His frown implied he had the same concern.

"I'll wrap it up. Give me just a moment," Artura said. She dragged a long sheet of brown butcher paper from a roll near the register.

It didn't matter where the other half of the team was. Brit headed toward the exit, confident the men would follow.

They stepped outside, and she nearly collided with Fumbles as he was pocketing his phone. "Kitten?" He stared at her in confusion.

Fuck.

"Hey." She gave him a bright smile. Her return was a portent of things to come, right? As long as he didn't think she should still be back on campus.

His gaze fell behind her. "Starkad?" His hand dropped to his holster.

Brit was faster, pointing the barrel of her pistol at his head.

CHAPTER SEVENTEEN

Kirby was rolling her eyes through a dramatic retelling of the Battle of Brávellir, when the library door swung open.

It's him. The words were instinct carried on years of fear, but Mark was dead.

It *was* Min, however. Despite his unfamiliar face, he was a welcome sight. His gaze passed over her as if she wasn't there—*appropriate*—and he approached the front desk. "Commander Gary asked me to deliver this." He handed the librarian an envelope.

She read the contents, then glanced at him. "Did he tell you what this says?"

"No. Commander asks me to do something, I do it."

"All right." The librarian stepped away from the desk.

Kirby glanced over her shoulder to see the woman disappear into the stacks, before turning back to her reading. Seconds turned into minutes—almost five—before the librarian returned.

She handed Min a book.

He saluted, thanked her, and was on his way.

The next day was a repeat. Min came in about an hour into Kirby's library time, handed the librarian a note, waited about five minutes for her to return with a book, and left.

Brit had never seen Erek in the library before. Not in the many years of knowing who he was. This wasn't just a set-up; it was a shitty one. What was Loki playing at?

After four days of the same, Kirby was as amused as she was curious. She and Min were being placed in the same spot, with just enough time to talk while they were *alone*. She'd like that. It would be nice to compare notes.

It would be nice to do other things, as well. As she stared at the pages in front of her, doing an incredible imitation of ignoring the private at the front desk, fantasy flooded her thoughts. Of Min's kisses. His touch, fingers rough and demanding as they roamed her body. The rush that came from his unique flavor of worship and pain. The way he felt, buried inside her.

She cut off the rambling thoughts before too much heat could flood her face. What was with her head? Nothing had changed between them from the time he gave her this face until now, but her heart was chanting his name almost as loudly as her body was.

Min was tender. He was kind. He treated her like a person—

Ah. Brit's feelings were bleeding into Kirby's. He'd been good to Brit. Even as a captor, he afforded her a dignity she never had outside of her relationship with Kirby. Brit didn't love him romantically, but she recognized he was attractive, and the bond of friendship forming between them was almost enough to make Kirby jealous.

The last thing she needed was to dive into the complications of her heart, especially with half her thoughts and emotions belonging to someone else. And she really didn't need her desire for Min to be spiraling out of control before the two of them had cleared a few things up.

None of that stopped the insistent pulse between Kirby's legs that wanted Min *now*.

She maintained the façade. A week dragged into two. Min's visits to the library weren't consistent, but most days, he was somewhere during her route. Kitchen patrol when she grabbed breakfast. Running laps with his company at the same time she jogged. And her Loki-assigned shadow was always present. If she decided she wanted a walk at 1 am—not unusual for Brit—he fell into line behind her.

Min probably had it worse. Grunts shared barracks, and he reported to someone else every minute of every day.

The novelty of a comfortable routine quickly faded into an ever-present cloud of oppression. Six years ago, this had been status quo for Kirby. Six months ago, it was Brit's life. Now, it was suffocating.

Getting out should mean *getting out*.

Day Fifteen in the library didn't yield anything more than the other days had. She was spinning her wheels in here. She needed a new approach. Not that she had any idea what direction to head. How long, until she had the freedom to roam near Hel's old office? If Loki'd had the place cleaned out, would it matter? Hel was supposed to be returning. He'd leave things intact, wouldn't he?

Time to head back to her apartment.

"*Kitten,*" Cyclops called her name from behind, and the warning bells in her head screamed. She spun to find him sprinting toward her. He stopped next to her, as calm as if he'd strolled the fifty meters between them. "A few of us are heading into town for coffee. Ice Queen, Venus, Melon-head. Everyone wants to catch up."

Her mouth practically watered at the idea of the local coffee shop's pastries. She'd prefer better company, but the thing about the Nobles was they were always kind to her face. She could tolerate that for an hour or two of freedom. "Do I get to lose the grunt?" She nodded toward her escort.

"Hey, Richard," Cyclops said.

"Sir?"

"Sergeant Brit is coming with us. You trust us to keep an eye on her, don't you?"

Richard nodded. "Yes, sir."

As if he was going to say anything else. *Freedom.* The light cloud spread through Kirby. Brit was more tentative, but willing to trade bullshit for a good brownie. "Thanks." She smiled warmly at Richard. He might be a grunt, but there was no reason to be rude.

She and Cyclops headed toward the parking lot, where the others were waiting at Ice Queen's

Jeep. The off roader was her baby; she'd spent a couple years restoring the hunk of junk she bought for fifty bucks from a guy in town.

She earned the nickname because she was so pale. Even in their pack of blond hair and blue eyes, she was an unearthly porcelain. And she always had to have her iced chai, even if it was minus ten. She'd even figured out how to reproduce her favorite drink the midst of a brutal winter training mission.

They all piled into the vehicle. There wasn't room for five people—not really—so Kirby sat on the back of the rear bench, her feet on the seat, and held on.

The drive into town was all laughter and jokes. Teams were paired based on a number of factors—complementary strengths and skill sets, and how they got along, were at the top of the list. Most teams would take a bullet for each other, but would also throw punches at each other in the heat of the moment. It was a balance between competition and friendliness, like so much in this place.

Ice Queen drove, with Venus next to her. Venus had earned her nickname after breaking her arm during training, but finishing the fight completely with her footwork. She was stone cold and still better than most, even without her arms. Just like the statue of Venus.

Cyclops and Melon-head sat on either side of Kirby. Melon-head got his name because, well... Cyclops caught him fucking a melon in the kitchen one night.

The wind in Kirby's hair felt amazing. The sun on her face... The carefree laughter and stories...

Kirby had never lived this life when she was here, but for Brit, it was familiar and phony. Was it really, though? They seemed so kind.

They're not, Brit's experience argued.

The other sniper teams had pulled away, the longer Brit was partnered with Mark—*Sadist*, for exactly the reasons his name implied—but in those moments when she found herself alone with any of them, they'd take the chance to remind her what kind of obstacle she was to their career.

She'd had as little a home here as Kirby did, but once Kirby was gone, she'd gone through it alone. Brit had spent more nights than not, lying in bed and staring at the ceiling, wanting to cry because Kirby was gone, and she was responsible. Because she wasn't strong enough to stand up to Mark. Because she chose her own status over the woman who loved her.

When they reached the coffee shop, the barista—DJ—greeted all of them and gave Kirby-as-Brit a warm *welcome back*. At least that seemed genuine. "Usuals?" he asked everyone before turning to her. "New salted-caramel chocolate brownies. You in?"

"Damn right." Kirby used her grin to beat back the painful memories. That was how Brit did it. She locked everything behind what mood she was supposed to be feeling, and let the mask talk.

Everyone reached for payment, but Venus got her card out first and handed it over. "'S'on me.'"

"I'll bring everything out in a few," DJ said.

The group took a table in the back. This time of day, the place was mostly quiet. The town did a lot of its business thanks to the campus, and early afternoon, class was in session and the people who lived here were working.

There was a bar down the street that always got noisy when Nobles or grunts showed up, but nobility tried to stay subdued in the coffee shop. It was half about appearances, and half because this was the only time they could really talk, and a lot of the things they said were meant for their ears only.

The light joking continued while they waited for their food and drinks, as if Brit had never left. As long as Kirby didn't look past the surface, the camaraderie was easy to fall into.

DJ dropped off their orders and faded back behind the counter.

Ice Queen leaned in close to Kirby. "Rumor is you're the reason Sadist didn't come back." Her voice was soft.

No thanks to any of you. "It's true. Dropped a bullet in the back of his head." Kirby wasn't bragging. It was what it was. Not that she felt any guilt.

A wave of *Thank Vidar* rolled around the table.

"In that case, how many of the other rumors are true?" Melon-head asked.

Kirby didn't know how much she could say, but the Brit part of her did. She had to offer a little resistance, though. "Is that the only reason you wanted me here?" she kept her tone light, despite the bitterness under the question. "To get the gossip from the source?"

"That, and you're single now. Sadist is gone. Valkyrie isn't here. If we court you, maybe one of us gets a three-person team. There's no way they're going to sideline talent like yours." Ice Queen spoke between sips of her iced chai.

"*Valkyrie,*" Kirby repeated. Apparently they'd given her a call sign after all. "It's so weird. Isn't it?" That Kirby was an actual Valkyrie.

"It's bullshit, if you ask me." Venus didn't like caffeine; she was having water and a cinnamon roll half the size of her head. "I know you and her... But she always thought she was better than us. Imagine if she'd found out who she was while she was still here."

Ice Queen rolled her eyes. "Ugh."

Well, ouch. Kirby didn't want the words to hurt, but they drilled a hole through her. Because they were true.

"Did you really run into her again?" Cyclops was a black-coffee-with-a-shot-of-espresso kind of guy.

Run into her... Let her become me... "Yup."

"I'm sorry, Kitten." Venus rested a comforting hand on her arm. "It doesn't seem right you got saddled with the psychos twice. But I know losing her hurt."

More than any of you will ever understand. Kirby's smile was weak. "Thanks." Brit *had* been crushed when she heard Kirby was dead. But these people thought the story Brit told in Kirby's trial was true. That Kirby had forced her into the relationship. And enough of Brit had felt overshadowed by Kirby,

173

even when she was gone, that it was easy to let the lie linger.

I'm so sorry, Brit's regret echoed loudly in Kirby's thoughts. "Hey, don't Blossom and Fumbles usually hang with you? I haven't seen them since I got back." Two weeks. Teams were rarely gone for more than a couple of days. And Brit actually liked Blossom and Fumbles. They'd seemed more genuine than most Nobles.

Melon-head cleared his throat. "Did Hel really make you immortal? Fuck Valkyrie. We want answers to the important questions." His order was identical to Kirby's. Caramel latte and brownie.

Why didn't he answer the question? Kirby nodded, and tugged down the shoulder of her T-shirt to expose a pale-white mark. "She did. I heal from everything I've encountered so far, but it still hurts like fuck, and if the wound is bad, it takes me out of things for a while. When I got back, Loki stuck a dagger in my shoulder."

Ice Queen traced the scar with her fingers. "It's barely visible, like it's been there for years. You returned the favor?"

Kirby scowled. "You know how slippery the fucker is, with that teleporting trick of his. I gave him a good run, though."

"Shame Hel didn't give you that gift too," Melon-head said.

"Speaking of, where have you been?" A more somber tone slid into Cyclops's question.

Everywhere. Nowhere. "Lost. I've been very lost. I went up against Kir—Valkyrie—with Hel. They killed her, and I thought they killed me. I woke up a few days later, but my head hasn't been in it. I wandered in a kind of fugue for a few months, and my brain finally cleared enough to find my way home."

"We're glad you're back." Ice Queen sounded sincere. *Actually* sincere, not *being polite* sincere. "I mean, yeah, because Hel said you'd return, but also because it's you. Welcome home."

"Thanks." Did they mean it? Kirby wanted to believe so, but Brit insisted she not be fooled. "So this prophecy about Hel's return. You're going to fill me in, right?"

Melon-head smirked. "You're going to love this."

Somehow she doubted that.

"Short version is, *death will bring back Hel.*" Ice Queen was always good at straight-to-the-point. "Blood spilled in her name is the sacrifice that gives her power."

Cyclops leaned in, elbows on the table, gaze locked on Kirby's. "She told us it would look like one of the Nobles betrayed her and died for it, but it wouldn't be true. That when they returned from the grave, it would be a sign that the next steps were imminent."

Did Hel know Brit was going to betray her in that fight? It seemed unlikely. She might have just as reasonably been talking about Kirby. What Hel meant didn't matter now; the Nobles' interpretation did. "She never told me any of this."

"Easier to make it look like you're a betrayer when you don't know the full story." Venus made the logic sound obvious. "But there's no reason you can't know now. We'll need your help."

"What are we doing? She told me things about everyone… going away, but she didn't give me many details." This wasn't how Kirby expected to find her information. It was almost too easy to be true. No reason to rule it out before hearing them out, though.

Cyclops crooked his finger, and everyone leaned in. This didn't look suspicious at all. "We spill the blood of the entire campus in her name." His voice was so low, Kirby wanted to believe she'd misheard him.

"I knew that much," Kirby said. Hearing it confirmed was still chilling. Especially with the way all of their faces shone with unwavering faith. "There's got to be more, or you would have done it already."

Melon-head managed a barking laugh encased in a whisper. Neat trick. "There's no elegance in that. We're waiting for more information about the *how*. We've been digging, though— literally and figuratively. A series of leylines intersect under the administration building, and in the foundations of every structure, there are a series of embedded runes. A giant seal or lock. We have to spill the blood correctly, to activate everything."

That sounded complicated for a plan that had built-in failsafes and would supposedly happen regardless of the steps taken to stop it. It also sounded gruesome. "We're not talking about a neat, clean, everyone-is-gassed-in-their-sleep kind of scenario?"

"No. It *has* to be messy." Cyclops almost looked sad. But the determined set of his jaw and hardness in his eyes never wavered.

"You said *the entire campus*. That means us, too." Kirby must be missing something. "After years of building all of this, she's going to burn it down to return? What's the point in creating it in the first place?"

Ice Queen's eyes sparkled. "That's the beauty of this entire thing. It's why your return is so critical. You prove death can be overcome. When Hel's back, she'll resurrect all of her true believers. We can't have the unfaithful on campus, though, because it will interfere with the final goal. That's why Blossom and Fumbles aren't here. They're on a long string of errands that only seem important." Conviction rang in her words.

In all of their words.

Telling them they were wrong and this was stupid threatened Kirby's cover and wouldn't convince them of anything.

CHAPTER EIGHTEEN

Brit didn't want to shoot Fumbles. It had been hard enough shooting a soldier, and she'd trained with this man for years. He was one of the few Nobles she actually liked.

He held both hands in the air but didn't re-secure his gun. "The others think your return means Hel's coming back too. I'm guessing none of them expect you to be with him."

The door behind Brit swung open, but she had to keep her focus on Fumbles.

"What the—"

Starkad trained his gun on Blossom, cutting her off. She moved into view, but unlike Fumbles, she'd drawn her weapon. "You made it back to Valkyrie." Blossom almost sounded jealous.

They'd given Kirby a call sign *after* she was gone? They called Brit *Kitten* and they gave a traitor one of the most revered names a person could carry. Okay, sure, Kirby actually was a Valkyrie, and they probably called her that sarcastically, but still... "Does it look like she's here?" Brit asked.

Pedestrians brushed around them on the sidewalk, never giving them a second glance, as if there wasn't a small pack of people pointing guns at each other.

"Neat trick, making the world ignore us," Fumbles said. "I didn't learn that one in class."

"You're welcome." Despite being the only one of them whose weapon was still tucked away, Gwydion looked more wound up than any of them.

Min had told Brit this was something Gwydion could do—make the world ignore things they didn't want to see. Watching it in action was far more impressive than she'd anticipated. He was a lot more powerful than he let on. No wonder Loki didn't like him.

"So… do we just stand out here and stare each other down?" Blossom asked. "None of us wants to deal with calling for dead-body cleanup in the middle of a busy sidewalk."

Fumbles looked at Starkad. "I'm going to assume what I say next won't backfire. I wasn't willing to die for Hel, and I'm sure as fuck not dying for Loki, now that she's gone." Far too quick a confession. He was lying. Wasn't he?

Brit didn't like the doubt. "We could all go someplace quieter and get a beer. Catch up. Talk about old times." She had spent a lot of luxurious time in the last few months, letting her true feelings show. Time to fall back onto her training and play things as cool as Blossom and Fumbles were.

These Nobles weren't walking away from this alive. If they went back to campus and saw another Brit there or told the others who they'd run into, it would put Kirby and the entire mission at risk.

But that didn't mean Brit was eager to execute them. Why couldn't Venus be here instead? Cyclops? At least it wasn't Dahlia. Brit didn't know if she could pull the trigger on her.

"There's a tapas bar around the corner." Fumbles nodded behind him.

Starkad gestured at Blossom. "Weapons away, and we'll go get lunch."

"You first." She sounded tenser than Fumbles.

Starkad holstered his gun.

Brit hesitated, for show. They didn't need to know she wasn't afraid of being shot.

Blossom applied the faintest pressure to the trigger as she stared Brit down. "You first, Kitten."

Kirby would be devastated if Starkad got shot.

He's immortal.

Oh, yeah. Brit holstered her pistol. As soon as her hands fell away, Blossom mimicked her motions.

"Lead the way," Brit said, hooking her arm through Blossom's like she would if they were back on campus and going for friendly drinks.

"I'm not holding his hand." Fumbles jerked a thumb at Starkad. "Dude still terrifies me."

Starkad's frustrated groan was priceless, and Brit was pretty sure he muttered *children* under his breath.

"Okay, Boomer," Fumbles said.

He had no idea.

Brit and Blossom took point. Easier to keep an eye on each other this way.

The bar was empty except for the bartender, and the waitress who took their order. Perfect place for talking. And execution if needed, but the knot in Brit's chest protested the thought of killing this team.

It didn't matter that the five of them sat casually around the table; tension radiated from their group, and all of them were half a heartbeat from drawing their weapons.

Fumbles sighed. "Along the same vein of making assumptions and confessions, when you didn't come back six month ago, we really hoped you'd gotten out."

"Why would you assume that I—" Brit swallowed the rest of her question. Asking was as good as an admission of guilt to anyone with TOM training. If Fumbles was sincere, though, honesty would work in her favor.

Blossom leaned in, one arm on the table and one still near her holster. "We saw what you were doing. I don't know if anyone else did, but Fumbles and I... They all thought—*think*—you're one of them. One of the loyal."

"I guess it takes one to know one," Fumbles said. "As in, you were doing the same things we'd planned. Getting rid of anything personal and replacing it with meaningless-but-pretty crap. You didn't live in your room, so much as use it as a place to sleep and hide."

The simple recognition struck gold on the truth of what Brit had been doing. "But you're still there."

"You waited for your opening. We need ours." Blossom flexed her fingers, and Fumbles covered her hand. "Leaving right after you, especially with the bedlam you threw the campus into by going and coming back and dying... We need things to be safer before we sever this tie."

"Let us walk away, like you did." Sincerity hung heavy in Fumbles's plea.

Starkad shook his head. "And have you go back? Tell everyone what you know? Confirm or deny any theories they have?"

"Then *let's all go talk someplace quiet* was a way to delay the inevitable. You always meant to kill us." Blossom didn't sound surprised. Just disappointed.

She had a point. Was there any way Starkad would let them walk away? He still hadn't let Brit leave. Except, he did once, and she fucked it up. Brit wanted to believe Blossom and Fumbles were sincere. That they'd fade into the woodwork, and no one would ever see them again. The way Brit should have done. Would have done, before she found out Kirby was alive.

Couldn't we let them go, this once? The plea stuck in Brit's throat. She'd need a better argument than that.

"Did you ever intend anything else?" Starkad asked.

Blossom shrugged. "There's always a glimmer of hope, you know? Maybe you don't. But it's the only thing that keeps those of us who don't want to be there going in that place."

"I'm sorry." Starkad sounded like he meant it.

Gwydion clenched his jaw. Would he argue? Something told Brit he wanted to.

Blossom unhooked her holster from her belt and set it on the table in front of her. "It's better than being there."

This wasn't right. It was actual surrender. Kirby's words echoed in Brit's thoughts. *I owe them the chance to face their attacker. To offer them an opportunity to change their minds.* What would Kirby have done if anyone took her up on her offer? If they did choose life and freedom over sacrifice servitude to Hel?

Brit shouldn't share her thoughts. Not in front of Blossom and Fumbles. But it was now or never, and she was tired of the regrets stacking up. "They deserve the same chance I had."

The glance Starkad gave her dripped with disbelief. "Not a great example."

"Please?" Fumbles asked. "Doing the same thing Blossom did. Putting my gun on the table."

Brit tensed, hand hovering over her holster, but Fumbles did as promised.

"You're not taking freedom from us." Blossom's tone shifted. Grew harder.

Brit swore time slowed to a crawl. Blossom reached for her holster, and Brit did the same, instinct taking over.

Blossom swiveled toward Starkad.

Kirby would be heartbroken.

Brit aimed and fired, hitting Blossom in the throat.

A bullet struck Brit in the shoulder, jerking her body and agony flared through her. She spun on Fumbles and fired three rounds. Two in the chest, one in the head, just like in practice.

Reality crashed around Brit, amplified by the ringing in her ears. Two of her former teammates were slumped half-out of their seats, blood pooling everywhere.

"*Fuck.* You've got another hole in you." Gwydion's exclamation mingled with her shock.

"Yeah. I need a cleanup." That was Starkad. Who was he talking to? "Spain. Cops will get here before you. I'm sorry."

Someone was tugging on her good arm. Taking the gun from her. Pulling her to her feet. *Gwydion.* "Come on."

Blossom and Fumbles were dead. They'd just wanted out, and now they were dead.

Brit followed Gwydion and Starkad through a shimmery portal, struggling to force numbness through her veins. It wasn't working. The ice wasn't there.

The bar vanished behind them, and they were back in the hospital wing at the palace.

"You have to stop using your body as a meat shield." Gwydion pointed her toward an exam table.

The bullet hadn't struck anything vital. As long as the shot was clean, it would heal before he could do much. Brit looked at Starkad. "Kirby would never forgive me if I let someone shoot you."

A smile lingered under his frown. "And she wouldn't have done any more damage than you did, when you tried to shoot me six months ago."

He's immortal, remember?

Apparently not. "Oh yeah." Brit sank onto the table, exhaustion rolling through her. They were dead. Gone.

"I'm with the doc. Try to put a slow down on stopping bullets with your body?" Starkad almost sounded concerned? "Hey." He crouched in front of her, drawing her attention. "They made their decision."

You're not taking freedom from us. Blossom's words ran on a loop in Brit's mind.

They had chosen, and Brit didn't regret that her instinct was to save Starkad.

That didn't make the loss of life—the loss of people who wanted a better life—any easier to process.

CHAPTER NINETEEN

Min was heading into town with a small group of soldiers from his company. They'd made top marks for five days in a row of drills, and earned a night of leave as a reward. A local bar was always friendly to the people from campus, and tonight was the perfect night to get drunk.

Rumor was, a group of Nobles would be there too. Most of his company hoped they'd pick up the tab tonight—Nobles made a lot more than grunts, and when they were drinking, they were happy to share the wealth.

Min was hoping to see Kirby in a less restrictive environment. Not that he expected he'd be able to pull her aside and chat. These people were always on their guard.

There were some things about being on TOM campus that Min enjoyed. The familiar brother- and sister-hood among the cadets and soldiers. Everyone here had formed a new sort of family. They ate, worked, played, and drank together. They even fucked together, despite it being against the rules. His roommate didn't hesitate to *sneak* his girlfriend in, whether or not Min was around.

And Erek had been as okay with the situation as Min was.

The thing Min disliked was the deception. Everyone here was lying about something, and it came as naturally as breathing to many of them.

Min didn't question when his commanding officer wanted him to deliver notes to the library. But Erek knew it was because Brit would be there. A manufactured errand meant to make one of them slip. Drop the façade. Give up who they really were.

The longer he shared a head with Erek, the more the reasons for constantly putting him in Brit's path made sense. He also understood more and more the *shoot first and ask questions later* mentality.

The schedule of it all didn't work for him, though. Erek hated routine, and this level of structure had never been part of Min's existence.

He also wasn't learning anything new about Hel, nor did he see any opportunities to do so. He was here to watch Kirby's back and help gather information. From his current position, he couldn't do either.

When they reached the bar, his fellow soldiers' cars already waited in the parking lot. There was also a Jeep and an El Camino. *Nobles.*

Min cheered with everyone else at the probability of *free beer*, and they headed inside.

The bar was like so many others Min had seen in his life—dimly lit, lots of tables, and groups of two or three locals who were probably here as many nights as they were home.

Everyone knew the elite members of Hel's Nobles. The part of him that was Erek was awed by them every time. Tonight, Ice Queen, Cyclops, Venus, Melon-head, Crazy Eight, Thrones, and Kitten were taking turns, buying rounds.

Kitten. Brit was anything but. And right now, she was laughing and joking with everyone else.

Except she wasn't Brit. Min saw the face, but when he looked at her, he also saw past the mask of the *ka*. Kirby's essence thrummed under the surface, in a way Min had never seen before. The two were fighting for dominance in the body. It must be a daily struggle for Kirby, to let Brit's instincts and memories take over. By now, there should be more of a blending.

As long as it wasn't putting her in harm's way, he wasn't concerned.

As Kirby exchanged quips with Ice Queen, her laughter sparkled through the room. But it wasn't nearly so bright in her soul. Min ached to join her group. To make her smile genuine and turn this into a night of celebration, like the festivals where his followers used to worship him.

Erek balked at the though. The sergeant, like all of the Nobles, was so far above him...

"Sergeant Brit is officially single." Venus's announcement carried over the voices, drawing everyone's attention. "And we think she should celebrate. Hook up with someone *fun* for a change. Who agrees?"

The soldiers hesitated, until the Nobles cheered, indicating it was okay to join in.

Erek remembered Mark. He hadn't known him personally, but everyone on campus believed the rumors about why he was called *Sadist*. They knew about Kirby, too, but she rarely interacted with them, and never with more than a passing regard. She didn't directly impact their lives any more than they did hers.

"I don't know," Kirby said. "It's been so long since I was single. What if I've forgotten how it works?"

When she said *single* she meant without a shooting partner, but it was common knowledge Mark considered her his property, and she and Kirby were a couple before that.

"Well, sweetheart, you just put your lips together and blow," one of the female soldiers called out.

Kirby strode toward her, mouth twisted in a playful smirk. "Are you volunteering to help remind me, Private?"

"I serve at your pleasure, sir." Tonight, rank and deference were words and nothing more.

Kirby trailed a finger along the private's lower lip, pulling it into a pout, then leaned in for a kiss that lasted several seconds and earned a round of cheers.

Min felt no jealousy for the moment; Kirby was playing a role. But the passion she elicited was tangible and alluring.

She stepped back. "I think it's coming back to me, but I'm not sure. Maybe someone else wants to help jog my memory about how this *kissing* thing works?"

She was met with more than half a dozen volunteers and didn't hesitate to sample every flavor. If she'd refused, it would expose her as someone other than a Noble having fun. Min hated that he not only saw the deception, but part of him also understood the rationale.

He wanted a taste as well. Both parts of him. Erek was happy to take a kiss without question, but Min would only give in if Kirby agreed. The question was, how to ask without destroying this façade they'd created?

*

Heat seared through Kirby when Min grabbed her wrist.

"Me next." His tone held no room for argument.

Kirby hid her reaction behind a playful mask, like she had been all evening, but her breath caught when he spun her to face him. It didn't matter that she saw someone else when she looked at his face; she felt the man underneath. The pull was hard to resist in the tamest of situations. Right now, everything inside her whimpered to drop the mask and give into the attraction.

"Rumor is, I'm in cahoots with you," she said.

"And yet, I'm not seeing any benefit from that." He held her gaze.

She could break out of this. *Brit* would break out of this. But if they were being watched anyway, maybe hiding wasn't the way to go. Perhaps they should be mocking the idea instead. "Are you looking for cahoots-with-benefits? Because that's not a thing."

"Make it one," someone in their group called.

"Kiss. Kiss. Kiss. Kiss." Their section of the bar erupted in the chant.

This was ridiculously childish. A college game, rather than a group of trained soldiers. Then again, Brit was twenty-five, and most of the others were younger because Kirby had taken out all of the older teams.

Holy shit. Realization mingled with Brit's confirmation, distracting Kirby from the moment. Brit had given Starkad the names of anyone with more experience who was a threat to her. She'd handed over the names of anyone who might be able to hunt her when she left.

Min tightened his grip, jolting her out of her head. "What do you say we give them what they want?"

"I'm in." *Gods,* she was in.

He knotted his fingers in her hair and crushed his mouth to hers.

Kirby ached to sink into the kiss. She missed his touch so much more than she wanted to admit. Min was there, distinct and familiar underneath Erek's touch. It took an immense effort to swallow her whimper amid a chorus of *Oohs.*

Brit would never yield control this way. Not here. Not to anyone but Kirby or Mark. She broke the kiss, fisted Min's shirt, and shoved him back onto a nearby bench. Kirby straddled his legs, putting her above him, and kissed him hard. When she dropped into his lap, his hardness pressed back.

She was barely aware of the whistles and cheers that erupted around them.

"I'd fuck you right here if I didn't think they'd try to execute me for it," Min murmured against her lips.

Crude, possessive words, that wrapped a grip around the *Kirby* part of her and kept it near the surface. "I'd let you." She had to push herself away and let Brit's *ka* have control again, to shove herself off his lap and regain her composure.

With the *Brit Show* peaking then losing its sparkle, everyone moved on to other conversations. Drinks flowed freely, until only the designated drivers in each group were talking without slurring their words. Including Kirby's shadow for the evening.

Loki was going to be furious.

"Hey, Kitten. We should head out." Ice Queen had an arm around Cyclops's waist and was responsible for keeping him upright.

Kirby didn't like the fuzz of alcohol, despite not having drunk much. She wanted to clear her head before returning. "Do you think anyone would mind if I walked back? Enjoyed the fresh air while I had it?" It wasn't a long hike. Less than eight kilometers. She ran more most mornings.

Ice Queen smiled. "We got your back. See you tomorrow?"

Kirby nodded.

Everyone left, and Kirby turned away from campus.

She'd stroll through town for a little while, and then head home. *Home.* The word made her

192

laugh. Campus was never Kirby's home or Brit's. Filled with peril and torture.

The kiss from Min lingered on her lips, even hours later. The rest of the exchanges were meaningless—a game. She had no doubt everyone involved felt the same. Here, sex was as much a weapon as an AUG was. A kiss didn't have any value.

Except with him. Kirby wanted answers. Needed this to end soon, so she could get back to her real home. Starkad. Gwydion.

Maybe even Min and Brit.

She never expected to think that again. Brit's sins were unforgivable.

But seeing the world through Brit's eyes painted everything in a new light. Suddenly, her choices, her fears, and even her betrayals, were understandable. Her guilt and regret were tangible.

Kirby didn't know how to reconcile the clash of what she'd believed with what she knew now about Brit.

At night, the town had a different feeling. An almost reverent calm settled over the streets, but an underlying danger ran through it. Kirby didn't know if she wanted to sink into the solitude or fight the unseen threat.

She approached a souvenir shop, and the trinkets in the windows caught her attention. A lot of turquoise jewelry. Leather. Things like dream catchers. The store window resembled a lot of the shops she'd seen in the southwestern US, but the artwork was unfamiliar. Silhouettes drawn in primitive shapes looked like they depicted death.

Violence. Blood spilling on the ground and life growing through it.

And two words repeated across all of the symbolic art. *Malsumis* and *Gluskab*.

Shoes scuffed on concrete. A body slammed into her side before she could react, pushing her into the side of a nearby building and knocking the air from her lungs.

CHAPTER TWENTY

Min was grateful Erek hadn't been a heavy drinker. He was a couple millennia old, and he'd never been drunk before, thanks to magic that kept chemicals from influencing him. Under many other circumstances, he might enjoy this new sensation of a light fuzziness in his thoughts, but the couple beers he'd had dulled his senses enough to slow his reactions.

The kiss at the bar lingered on his lips and in his thoughts. The gathering tonight was similar to those ancient days of worship, and his queen was still in town, on foot. He wanted more of Kirby before he returned to base, and he had an idea. It was a shitty one, but enough of Erek was in control that it felt smart.

"Hey." Min slapped his palm against the back of the driver's seat, interrupting a tirade about how much it sucked to be the designated driver. "Pull over. I need to take a leak."

"Are you kidding me? Hold it."

"I tried, man. Pull over, or I'll wet the seats."

The car drifted to the side of the road. "Hurry. I'm tired," the driver barked. He had a name, but Erek could never remember it. Save for a couple close teammates, most of these guys were *Private* to him.

Min stumbled a few meters away from the shoulder, far enough to be out of *falling water* ear range, and waited a few seconds before calling, "Aw, fuck. I pissed on my shoes." He was prepared to *actually* do so, if needed, but he was hoping the threat would be enough.

"What? Fucking moron." The irritation in the driver's voice was sharp and potent. "I don't want your piss-covered shoes in my car."

"You can't leave me here." Min hoped they'd do exactly that.

The rear car door slammed shut. "Can and am. Enjoy the walk back to base, piss-shoes." The vehicle pulled away.

That actually worked? Min smiled in the darkness. Now, he'd wait. Aside from cutting through fields, this was the only road back to campus. If he hung out here, Kirby would be along soon. It was a reckless idea, but Erek did stupid shit like this on a regular basis, especially for pussy. It was the main reason he was a grunt—he had top scores in handgun marksmanship and observation, but he couldn't keep his dick in his pants, and he didn't try to hide it.

Half an hour passed, and there was no sign of Kirby. If he headed into town to look for her, he ran the risk of missing her. But he wasn't sitting out here all night waiting.

****

When a hand clenched around Kirby's throat, pinning her to the wall, she gasped with already-short breath.

Davyn? She stared into the haunting gaze of the berserker. Her mind ticked through options to break free of his grip. His reach was longer than hers. He had her on the tip of her toes, so she didn't have any leverage in her feet. He was using a single hand. She could drive her arm into his and risk breaking her own.

"Whoever you are, I don't have what you want," she croaked.

His grin was two terrifying rows of teeth. He'd let enough bear out to increase his muscle mass and bulk. "You know exactly who I am. I'd love your life, in exchange for the one you tried to take."

Fuck. Because Brit had been sent to kill Azzie. "I never intended to take that shot." Kirby sank into Brit's memories, the way Min had advised her.

"I want your life, but I can't take it until I have something more important," he growled. "I want Loki."

"Take a number?" Kirby could play games. Pretend he was asking for a fictional person. But he'd picked her for a reason, and too much taunting would earn her a crushed windpipe. She filled her lungs with as much air as she could, lifted her feet off the ground to kick off the wall, and aimed a foot at his gut.

He let go, to step out of reach.

She landed on the ground, rolling into the fall to charge forward instantly. There weren't a lot of soft targets on Davyn, and the big ones were around center mass. A blow to his diaphragm or balls would suit her fine.

He sidestepped and slammed an elbow into her back.

Stars danced in front of her eyes. The asshole was faster than she remembered. "I can't give you anything." She should reason with him. At least long enough to catch her breath. "You walk onto that campus, and they'll shoot you on sight."

"You *can* give me something. You can get me close to him." He lunged for her again.

Kirby needed to evade as much as possible. Brit couldn't take on a berserker. Even on a good day, with access to everything-Valkyrie, Kirby would struggle. "How?"

"You'll walk me through the front gate."

Laughing was the worst possible idea right now. She needed to take this fight off the streets. If some well-meaning person came along and tried to help the little lady in distress, Davyn would pulverize them.

Brit probably wouldn't handle the situation this way, but he didn't know that, and Kirby was holding onto mental control for this fight. "You missed the part about being shot on sight," she said.

"I'll take my chances." His jaw and nose shifted, and he dropped onto all fours, leaning closer to *bear*.

Shit. She definitely didn't want anyone coming along now. With her next evasion, she angled herself toward a nearby alley. "I'm not talking about a single bullet. They'll rain assault-rifle rounds down on you until you stop."

"You're stalling."

"I'm being honest." One more step, and they'd be off the street.

Davyn roared and leaped past her, blocking her path. His backhand was more paw than hand, slamming into her chest and scraping claws across her arm enough to let the blood flow freely. "Don't try to corral me."

That broke a rib or two. *Fuck.* She wasn't getting her breath back for a little while. This had to stop. "Ill is it to leave the right undone." Words from Kirby's first life. A berserker prayer, spoken before battle. A phrase that was as much hers as Starkad's back then.

"Where did you hear that?" Davyn paused, but his body was still coiled, as if to spring at any moment.

Every inhale made her grit her teeth. "I don't want Azzie dead." Would Brit know the woman's name? Her association to Davyn? Yes. She'd hunted them.

"Bullshit. You were sent to kill her. I tracked you for days after, until you vanished. Tell me. Where. Did. You. Hear that phrase?"

If she told Davyn who she was, she might be able to convince him. She knew things about him that no one else alive had ever seen. But the risk of consequence for revealing herself to *anyone* was too high. "If I tell you that, they're not going to let *me* back on campus, either. I'm no good to you that way.

I'll tell you how to get in without going through the front gate, but you have to promise not to do it without me."

Davyn's smile was all teeth. "You can barely breathe. You're not in a position to negotiate."

"This isn't a matter of give and take. It's reality."

"It's convenient bullshit. As soon as I let you go, I lose this chance. You stumbled into my path. I'm not giving up this opportunity." At least he wasn't attacking any more. Some of his more beastly features were retreating, but the bear stayed near the surface.

Gods, she missed Starkad. "Fine. Waterside of the school, there's a spot on the beach…" She gave him specific instructions. "But hear me out before you decide to use it, because my way is safer." The pain was easing in her chest. Wow, this fast-healing thing of Brit's wasn't bad. It wasn't as good as Kirby's, but still…

"You're talking a lot, for someone who doesn't say anything."

"Yeah, yeah. Call Starkad. Tell him everything that just happened. Meet me back here in one week, and I'll get you an audience with Loki." Could Kirby meet that deadline? She had no idea. But Starkad would explain things to Davyn, and that should buy her some time.

His growl was still part-bear, part-human. "If I don't like what he has to say to me, I'll find you again. I know you're here."

"I swear to you in Týr's name, I'm giving you as much as I'm able." If Hel were still here, she'd have Brit's head, for invoking a god who wasn't associated with TOM.

"Do you truly know what that oath means?"

Kirby nodded. Honor in battle. Honor in death. Honor above all else.

"All right," Davyn said. "One week, unless I don't like what Starkad has to say."

Relief coursed through Kirby, as she watched him walk away. TOM soldiers might not respect the old traditions, but at least someone did. *Please let him still be the same bear I knew, so long ago.*

The Brit part of her argued that she'd made a massive fucking mistake.

CHAPTER TWENTY-ONE

Min found Kirby a few blocks from the bar, sitting on the sidewalk with her back up against an empty storefront.

"You shouldn't be here." Her greeting was tired.

He knelt in front of her. Fading bruises on her neck, as if she'd been choked, glared at him. Concern sped through him, and he brushed his fingers gently over the marks. "What happened?"

"You first. You're jeopardizing everything by being here." Kirby closed her hand around his. Her touch was warm and firm. Familiar and right.

Her condition reinforced his desire to be here, by her side. "I pretended to pee on my shoes. Driver wouldn't let me back in the car." Erek was smug over the simplistic plan.

Her smile reaching her eyes was worth the story. "How long before they ask where you are?"

"Your turn. What happened? Wait. Hold that thought." He headed down the nearby alley and checked a side door. Locked. He gripped the knob, pressed toward the opposite side of the frame, and leaned his shoulder into the door. It gave after a second shove.

He returned to scoop Kirby into his arms.

"I can walk just fine." Despite her protest, she draped her arms around his neck. "You're lucky you didn't trigger any alarms."

"I'm hoping my luck runs a little longer." He carried her inside the empty shop. Newspaper covered the front windows, and dust coated the floor and the sheets draped over cases. He set her on her feet, yanked a drop cloth off a steel counter, and lifted her to sit. "Talk to me."

She scrubbed her face. "I ran into an old friend of Kirby's. I can't tell you much more, without it being dangerous to Erek, but my ribs are healed now, so I'm doing much better."

"Ribs?"

"He's a berserker. Please don't ask more. Why are you here? Not that I'm complaining. I'm so glad you're nearby, even when we can't talk, but…"

He grasped her fingers. The last few months apart vanished in here. He knew why she'd sent him away. There was no longer any question. This wasn't the time to discuss it, but his need to be close to her was overwhelming. "I'm here to protect you."

"I don't…" She laughed lightly. "That's sweet."

"You don't need me watching over you. I realize that." He kissed her fingertips. *Worship her.* Urd's voice, words he'd forgotten for centuries, echoed in his head. "But last time I watched you die, I swore it would be the *very* last. I have to try."

Kirby rested her hand on his cheek. "I hate seeing you in this face. Hate hearing your words in someone else's voice."

"As soon as we're done, we can go back to being us." He didn't hate looking at Brit's face, but he would show more hesitation if he couldn't see past the surface, to the real person underneath. Inspiration struck. "Close your eyes."

She did as commanded.

He stripped off his shirt, folded it, and tied it in place as a blindfold. Her playful smile and the way she brushed her fingers over the cotton, tugged at his desire and amplified his need to feel her.

The kiss from the bar hovered at the front of Min's mind, pushing him to claim her mouth. Her moan against his lips was intoxicating. The connection tugged at centuries of love and desire, but the feelings filtered through the lens of Erek. Min dove deeper into the kiss, tangling his tongue with Kirby's. Devouring the spice of the moment.

This wasn't the first time he'd been intimate in a different body, but he'd never tasted this flavor of passion. This burning need to be part of another person.

He dragged his fingers up her spine, shoving her shirt out of the way in the process, and dipped his head to cover her stomach in kisses. To lick up to her breasts, along the top of her bra.

This was forbidden. Against the rules. Sex had never been forbidden for Min before.

He fumbled to undo her jeans and shoved them to the ground.

Kirby giggled when the clothing got caught on her boots. "Shoes come off first."

"I knew that." Min did. Erek had forgotten, in his eagerness to taste this gorgeous woman. It was such a pure, raw sensation. He trailed his tongue along her thigh, as he bent to unlace her boots. "Step out."

Kirby rested her hands on his shoulders for balance, as she stepped out of each shoe. She was barely upright when he stood, gripped her hips, and lifted her onto a nearby countertop.

He yanked her bottoms off the rest of the way, not caring where they landed, and knelt at her feet. Min wanted to give her immeasurable pleasure. Erek was hungry to bury his face between smooth thighs and taste her.

He dragged his tongue up her slit. Her groan was the perfect reward. He dove in with enthusiasm, licking and sucking. Memorizing the flavor of her juices on his tongue. Nibbling her clit until she squirmed. Sliding two fingers inside her and pumping, until she came, knotting her fingers in his hair and holding him in place to grind against his face.

Min pulled away when Kirby's shudders of pleasure slowed. Desire as a mortal was unique. His erection dug into his zipper as he stood. His pulse hammered in his ears, and his heart against his ribs.

He crushed his mouth to Kirby's again, falling into the softness of her lips and the hunger in her kisses. Her enthusiasm matched his, as they shared her flavor. Her energy sang underneath it, showing him her soul, rather than her body. Letting him experience everything that was Kirby.

If he were himself, he'd have poetic words. "I need to fuck you." Not flowery, but honest and effective.

She made quick work of his zipper, and his anticipation spiked when she wrapped her hand around his shaft to free him.

He shoved between her legs without further fanfare, and thrust inside her. That first penetration was heaven, her heat drawing him in.

She wrapped her legs around his ass, setting a fast pace he was happy to match. Her slick warmth drew him to the edge of climax within moments, and he lost himself in the sensations. Pounding. Slamming inside her. Experiencing everything at once.

He came hard, the night sky exploding behind his eyelids. It was over too soon. He wanted to keep feeling Kirby.

He kept up the pace until his cock started to soften, then slowed to a stop, planting his hands against the counter on either side of her, to stay upright.

Min didn't know how long he stood there, Kirby wrapped around him, their breathing the only sound keeping them company in the abandoned shop.

"We need to get back to campus." Her voice was reluctant.

She was right, but he wasn't ready to go yet.

Kirby nudged his shoulders to push him back. "We've already been missed. I'd love to stay here forever, but we can't."

"I know." His reply was heavy. An ache grew in his chest at the thought of walking away from her. It wasn't as though he'd never see her again, but that tiny little voice saying he'd lost her too many times was reluctant to walk away from her tonight.

CHAPTER TWENTY-TWO

Kirby clung to the stolen time with Min, burning it into her heart as she walked back to campus. It wasn't a resolution in their relationship—they had a more roads to cross for that—but the connection… She'd missed having that with him.

As she drew within sight of the front gates, a spotlight came on, blinding her and sending her stomach into her shoes.

"Sergeant Brit. Lie on your stomach on the ground, arms on the back of your head and legs spread." The command blared over a loudspeaker.

She dropped to the pavement without hesitation. This was the reception she expected when she first came back. Why now? Her pulse hammered in her ears. Was Min here? The reckless night may have fucked them twice.

"Do not move." Bossy fucking voice.

Two pairs of boots moved into her field of vision, but she heard additional footsteps and had no doubt at least three guns were trained on her from a distance.

Another boot landed in the small of her back. Her hands were jerked back, jarring her shoulders.

She was yanked to her feet, and a bag was roughly shoved onto her head, blocking her view. The frisk for weapons was rough and thorough. *Buy me dinner before the body cavity search?* Not the time, no matter how much she wanted to taunt someone as a way to ignore her fear.

Kirby was half-led, half-dragged to a bench seat in what would be a Jeep, and the vehicle jerked forward. The hands on her arms kept a tight grip the entire time, and other legs locked hers in place.

This was severe, even for TOM. A bitter cocktail of bile and tequila burned up her throat.

The ride didn't last as long as she expected. Standard practice was a loop around campus, before landing back at the facility near the entrance. Then again, all of this was a degree off center from *procedure.*

The Jeep stopped, and she was dragged to a new location, the toes of her shoes bouncing roughly against the ground, with no chance for her to find her footing.

They walked for several hundred meters, up stairs and around corners, before she was shoved into a chair and a door latched shut behind her. Then, there was silence.

A latching door meant this wasn't the interrogation room. She shifted in her padded seat and was greeted with a wooden creak and chair legs that scraped against a carpet or rug.

If they were going to torture her in a traditional way, a carpeted room was an odd place to do so, but TOM didn't do traditional torture. They'd use honey over vinegar unless they saw no other choice.

The knowledge didn't stop her heart from slamming against her ribs. Would she have to blow her cover? Would she have time to decide before she was unconscious?

The ties on her wrists went taut, then fell away, and her hood was ripped off.

She blinked several times in the subdued lighting of Loki's office. He leaned against his desk, across from her, arms crossed and hood in one hand.

Silence was her best option until he gave her more. She'd stare him down all night if she had to. Or part of the night. Or maybe a few minutes. Brit hated waiting out situations like this.

"Not many people go hand-to-hand with a berserker and live to talk about it," he said.

Fuck. "The average high in Salt Lake City in June is eighty-point-two degrees Fahrenheit."

He raised an eyebrow.

Kirby shrugged. "Are we not swapping random facts?"

"I've been spinning bullshit for centuries, practicing the fine art of deception, and yet Brit always impressed me with hers." Loki dropped the hood on his desk and rested his palms against the edges, gaze never leaving hers. "But you... Lying is one of those things you don't have a gift for. Kirby, isn't it?"

Every muscle in her body tensed without permission, and her drink threatened to repeat on her. It didn't taste nearly as good the second time around.

She was never touching tequila again. "Brit. B-R-I-T. I know we all look alike, but it can't be that hard to tell me from a dead woman."

"Valkyrie. Resurrected, which you told me yourself that you knew."

"But I prefer the term *dead woman*." Kirby could do this with him for hours when she was Brit, but he'd figured out the truth, and she doubted any amount of banter would dissuade him. How did he find out? She'd slipped several times. Which one busted her? Who else knew?

He drummed his fingers on the underside of the desk's lip. "You're not going to ask the questions you want to, because you think it will make you look guilty. I'll tell you anyway. I've known the two of you were a lie since Not-Erek walked in the front gates. Don't worry, his cover is safe. I'm as unfond of Hel's Nobles as they are of me."

Kirby wasn't reassured. Why had she taken for granted that Loki let her back onto campus so easily? Because she was still free to roam. *Idiot.* "You're feeling a little *Evil Villain Monologuing*, but I thought we were on the same side."

"I'd like us to be. How is Kirby, by the way?"

"Alive? Fucking a couple of immortals? Really high strung and self-destructive?" The Brit part of her knew that was the expected answer, despite not meaning it. The reality of the words gnawed at Kirby's core. "Do you want me to provide a psychoanalysis, or are you looking for some other kind of answer?"

"I'm not in the mood for games. I'm being straight with you, because I'm hoping you'll give me the same."

Kirby twisted her mouth in disbelief. The immediate threat had lessened. She was loose. Danger was directly in front of her. If he moved or vanished, she could react. Might as well let him talk. "Maybe you're the imposter, in that case."

"Heh." His laugh was flat. "I know Brit was in the warehouse. That she was part of the rescue mission. An unexpected part, but what a fun surprise."

"What warehouse?" Was any of Brit's life private? Had he somehow been following her this entire time? No. Gods were capable of a lot of things, but none of them were omnipresent.

"The faithful will return."

Ice raced down Kirby's spine, courtesy of Brit's memory. "Creepy. Is that a new thing we're doing?"

"I was him. The man she shot. I saw the entire thing. Which is how I knew your story about wandering the world in a fugue was bullshit." He leaned close and dragged his nose up the side of her neck. "But fuck if you're not a near-perfect replica."

"Dolly Parton once lost a Dolly Parton look-alike contest." She wasn't fooling anyone, but pride and training—and a lot of *what next*—kept her from admitting Loki was right.

"I can't figure out whose magic this is," Loki said. "But your attitude… Too flippant for the berserker. Too lethal for the trickster. Too well integrated to be anyone but another of our fine, upstanding graduates."

"Thanks to Hel, we're in a class of our own."

"That means you're Kirby. It must kill you to see how much they love Brit and how much disdain they had for you. Does the reminder of your failure destroy you? Utterly and completely?"

Did he really think anyone here gave a fuck about Brit, beyond what she could do for them? Thank the gods Brit was a master at masking her emotion, because Kirby wanted to crack. To grab that letter opener off Loki's desk and jab it in his throat. It wouldn't kill him, but it would convey her irritation.

"Now that I've laid all my cards on the table—"

"I doubt that," Kirby said.

Loki *tsked.* "You keep pretending I'm wrong, and I'll know I'm right. Here's the deal. I'm not going to kick you out or blow your cover. As far as anyone is concerned, you and I had this aggressive talk because you needed to convince me you're being honest about your reasons for being here. You did. In return, you'll share anything you learn with me."

"Learn about...?"

"This big plan of Hel's to bring herself back, and kill everyone here in the process."

That was direct. "Looking for a path to your own resurrection?"

"I'd rather not hit the *dead* point to begin with." Loki's tone was flat. "I helped build this place for a reason. Destroying everyone means I no longer have access to this resource. I'm making the big assumption that you'd like to stop this—Kirby never liked unnecessary death. We both have something to gain from this."

It was a good assumption, and she was too twisted up in what did and didn't look like admitting he was right, to know how to reply. What he said made sense, though. This was Hel's plan, not his. Loki was one thing above all else—in everything for himself.

"Tell me why," she said. "What do these people give you that you can't get anywhere else?"

"Same thing you've always offered—they destroy potentials."

One, in particular. The woman prophesied to bring about his destruction. "You'd utilize an entire school, to get rid of one little girl?"

"Not the entire school. The Nobles don't serve me, and they're going to have to go. But Starkad used it to find one single girl, and I doubt you're complaining."

Not technically true. Starkad had been here long before Kirby. Her arrival was lucky for both of them.

The Nobles were Hel's trusted executioners. If Kirby told Loki that, if she let him take them out of the picture, would that stop anything? She'd like to believe so, but that was the problem—she didn't know. Hel's plan was supposed to be foolproof, and removing a handful of people from the equation hardly seemed like a groundbreaking idea. At least without more information.

"You're undecided still," Loki said. "I've given you enough information that you could walk out of here right now and organize a coup against me."

"Or this is a game, before you remove me from campus or feed me to my colleagues."

He sighed. "In Wales, when you and I fought in the field—*you* being Kirby, because you haven't changed my mind—I was responsible for the driver dropping you there. You know that already. But I did it to talk to you about this. About what Hel was planning. I picked the open field to minimize casualties. You people are really shoot-first, ask-questions later."

"We do teach that here," Kirby said. "A phone call wouldn't work? A request for an in-person meeting?"

Loki stared at her for a moment, lips pursed. "Is it working now? I wasn't responsible for the fae who were captured, and neither was Hel. Bad timing on the part of another board member. I was the one who gave the information to Aeval about where to find them. And I was there at the warehouse to make sure everyone got out okay. Turned out I didn't need to step in."

"This is all really convenient. Assuming I know what you're talking about." *And you could have stepped in sooner.* What was Kirby supposed to do with this *confession*? Was that even what it was?

"You're thinking I could have stepped in sooner. Yeah, it's true. Important people lived. You could have told me who you were when you arrived on campus, and you didn't. It's all about keeping up appearances."

It all made sense, at least as far as his motivation was concerned. She didn't buy the, *here's every time I tried to do right by you,* wrapped in a neat little package. That was an entire string of implausible coincidences. "Let me see if I understand this. You're really the good guy—"

"I never said that."

Honesty. Wow. "Fair enough. Basically, you're proposing we work together to keep as many people here alive as possible, so you can continue to hunt... her."

"And so you can say you saved lives. I'm even willing to make a trade with you, as a gesture of good faith."

Kirby saw a billion different loopholes in this conversation, but she needed a way to move forward, and he might be it. "What kind of trade?"

"Introduce me to the berserker who tore up your clothes—don't deny that; you're stained with his magic, and I know my enemies—and I'll pull your shadow from you."

Davyn wanted to meet Loki anyway. This was an easy way to deliver. "You can still watch me, even without a shadow."

"Not when you head into town."

She was about to yield. To make a deal with the devil. "Which you'll keep track of."

"You're a smart girl, regardless of which one you actually are. You can buy yourself whatever time you need."

"I'll take the trade, but I have to think about the rest. I'm still not admitting anything."

Loki grinned. "We both know you don't have to."

Kirby hated this. Would his drive for self-preservation really keep him from turning on her? Only as long as she served his purposes.

CHAPTER TWENTY-THREE

Starkad didn't know what to do with himself. He wasn't used to being the one waiting at home for answers, and it was making him twitchy. He'd paced the castle for a few days, until Aeval told him he made the other occupants uncomfortable.

In the past, he'd filled his days with drinking, fighting—wars or otherwise—teaching, espionage for the highest bidder…

After he pulled Kirby out of TOM, he had her company. Brit's leads to verify.

She was the other thing nagging his thoughts. What happened in Spain could be interpreted a lot of different ways, but he kept coming back to the most obvious explanation—Brit's actions were exactly what they looked like on the surface. Her first instinct had been to save his life, for Kirby, at the cost of her own and those of her former associates.

Starkad wasn't interested in practicing with her; he didn't have the same indoctrinated need to always be at his sharpest, that TOM embedded in its students.

Gwydion was taking meals with Brit now. Starkad could join them.

Those thoughts led him back to the dark corner of his mind he didn't care for. The one Brit dusted off with her questions.

His drive to tear her down my have lessened after Spain, but that didn't mean he wanted her company.

Starkad's phone rang. he didn't recognize the number that popped up. Not unusual—people from Urd liked their privacy. "Yeah," he answered, excited at the prospect of something to do.

"Starkad." Davyn pronounced his name in a way Starkad hadn't heard in centuries.

"What can I do for you?" Polite formalities were never their thing back in the day. And this was the second time, talking to Davyn in just a few weeks, when they hadn't seen each other previously since *back in the day*. It made Starkad uneasy.

"We need to meet."

Definitely not a good sign. "Why and where?"

"Upstate New York. How soon can you get here?"

Near TOM. This kept getting worse. "Why are you there? Why do you want me there?"

Davyn sighed. "I need to get onto that fucking campus. The one the gods own."

"Don't do that. They'll shoot you. A lot." Starkad's immortality was a gift from Kirby. He didn't know what had kept Davyn alive all this time, but it probably wasn't Valkyrie magic.

219

"Yeah. That's what the girl told me too," Davyn said.

"What girl?" Had the idiot already tried to head onto campus, and this was him, forced to call—

Starkad dismissed the thought. Davyn wouldn't be forced to do anything.

"Brit. The one who told me to call you. After she said, *Ill is it to leave the right undone.* She told me if I talked to you first, she'd help me get onto campus."

Kirby. Starkad had so many questions. How did she look? Was she all right? Did Davyn hurt her? If so, it wouldn't matter what kind of immortality he had; Starkad would obliterate him. "I don't know if that's a promise she can keep."

"Can you meet me or not?"

"Is she okay?" Starkad shouldn't ask. He couldn't help himself.

"She's fine. Resilient as fuck."

Thank the gods. "I can be wherever you want." Wait. That was a bad idea. "You didn't bring Azzie there, did you?" So close to Loki, the god who would do anything, to keep that girl from killing him?

"No. She's with Finn. I don't plan on being here long." Davyn gave him a town name that was a couple of hours from the TOM campus, and an address. "Can you be there in a few hours? I'd rather look you in the eye when we talk. "

A sentiment Starkad understood. "Yes."

Davyn probably wasn't a threat, but Starkad had no doubt the bear would do *anything* to protect his ward. Not just because of the oath. Being protectors was in berserkers' blood as much as violence was.

Starkad wasn't going so close to TOM without someone skilled, watching his back. How much did he trust Brit?

She'd given him large quantities of good intel in the past. She'd taken bullets on their behalf several times.

She'd also tried to kill him. Watched someone else try to kill Kirby.

In other words, she probably wouldn't shoot him in the back, but that didn't mean he had to like her.

Brit wasn't in her room.

Starkad began a systematic sweep of the palace. Nothing as intense as what they'd done in the warehouse, but just as thorough.

When he reached the back end of the main floor, a large splash of sunlight across the marble drew his attention. One of the double doors leading outside was wide open.

The fresh air and warmth drew him toward the garden. A rainbow of wildflowers lined the lazy stone path he followed. The weather wasn't always perfect here, but it was close. Maybe he should spend more time outside.

Laughter drew his attention, and he changed direction, cutting across a lawn of clover and wild grass.

"I assume every single one of his, intentional or otherwise, has a deep, significant meaning," said Gwydion. He sat on a blanket, half-turned away from

Starkad, printouts of the book interior from the shop spread out in front of him.

Brit sat next to him. She rested her weight on her arms, behind her, and her legs were stretched out in front of her. "He does strike me as that kind of guy. Then again, so do all of mine. I just don't have as many."

What were they talking about?

Gwydion flipped back and forth between two of the photos. From here, they were recognizable. The only two in the set that might refer to Hel, but neither Starkad, nor Gwydion, nor Brit could figure out how.

"With the number of new bullet holes in you, one might think you were trying to catch up," Gwydion said.

Ah. Scars.

"You didn't answer for yourself." Brit turned her face toward the sunshine. Her voice was lighter than Starkad had ever heard it.

"Some of them, I got for deeply personal reasons. To commemorate a time or place or person." Gwydion sighed. "Others I got because they were pretty or the design amused me." He tugged up his shirt sleeve and pointed to his bicep. "I got this one in Kuwait, after drinking some of the worst moonshine ever—"

"Do you get drunk?"

Not just scars. Tattoos as well.

"No." Gwydion shook his head. "But there's a habit and a ritual in drinking, especially when imbibing something homemade by soldiers. I've had some bad hooch in my lifetime, but this stuff was utter shit. I wanted a different memory, to wash that one from my mind, and we found a tattoo parlor downtown. Kirby liked the dichotomy of the butterfly resting on the thorns."

That did sound like Kirby. It was odd to observe this exchange. Starkad had watched Brit grow up and become this, via Kirby, but he'd never seen her outside the bubble of TOM, even after she left. Out here, it was easy to see how she'd deceived Min and Gwydion into thinking she wasn't a threat.

"So is this the first kind or the second?" Brit traced along Gwydion's arm.

"Until you asked that, I would have said it was the *because it amused me* kind. Now I'm not so sure."

Brit tilted her head back, as if looking at the sky. "Is he right? Do all of your scars have an intensely personal meaning?"

She was talking to Starkad. She probably heard him approach.

"Every single one of them." He didn't want to get sucked into this nostalgia, or whatever it was. First Min had decided Brit was trustworthy, and now this. Was there an opposite to Stockholm syndrome, where the captors came to adore the prisoner? "Are you up for another, probably less dangerous mission?"

Brit sat up and twisted on the blanket, to face him. "No getting shot?"

"I almost guarantee it." Though Davyn might go for her throat if she pissed him off. Not that Davyn needed to see her. "We're meeting an old acquaintance of mine, and I need you to watch my

223

back. Stay unseen. We'll only be a few hours from campus, so discretion is crucial."

Her laugh was tinged with sarcasm. "No shit. I notice you didn't say *friend*. You don't have a lot of those, do you?"

"Observant. That's why I'd like you there." No reason to rise to the bait.

"Do I get to know who we're meeting?" she asked.

"His name is *Davyn*."

She raised her brows. "Big bear of a guy? Thing for redheads?" It made sense she knew who he was. She'd hunted Azzie.

"That's him. He's literally a bear, and she's his ward, nothing more."

"Mhm. You ever tell anyone that about Kirby? *She's just my ward*."

More times than he cared to admit. This wouldn't be a repeat of the conversation in the bookstore, where Brit had gotten under his skin. "This is a very different situation."

"Right. There are really two of you still left alive? Do I need to worry about him smelling me or anything?"

"You don't smell the way you used to." Starkad didn't have a hypersensitive sense of smell, but it was heightened, especially when he shifted. Enough to tell people apart by their scent.

Brit sniffed her hand. Under her arms. "I don't smell like rotting flesh, do I? Is it getting worse?"

Gwydion sniffed her. "You smell fine to me."

"You don't stink; you just don't smell the way you used to. Are you interested in joining me or not?"

Brit hopped to her feet. "I'm in."

"We're leaving as soon as you're ready." Starkad wanted time to survey the area, and Brit would as well. A *yes* about ten minutes earlier would have been nice. It was a good thing Davyn didn't ask to meet immediately.

Brit didn't take long to change. Starkad handed her a gun. He hoped it wouldn't be necessary, but that it would matter if it was needed.

She looked surprised, but secured the weapon without commentary.

Gwydion dropped them off a few blocks from the meeting location, and Starkad and Brit began a sweep of the area.

The ground rumbled under their feet, and rattled all the windows on the street. An earthquake? Here and now?

A familiar growl sounded behind them. *Shit.*

"*You.*" Davyn's voice was barely human. "You lied to me."

Starkad stepped between Brit and a snarling Davyn, as they all faced each other.

CHAPTER TWENTY-FOUR

Kirby didn't know how much she could trust of what Loki said, beyond his desire to keep an entire personal army at his beck and call. Her shadow was gone, but large portions of the campus had cameras. She felt less safe the day after talking to Loki than she had since she arrived. She skipped range practice and jogging, partly to not have to face so many unknown variables, and partly to see if the change in schedule drew anyone's attention.

Someone knocked.

There it was.

She answered, and was surprised to find Ice Queen and Venus, dressed in camouflage. Hooray.

Not.

"What's with the BDUs?" Kirby asked.

Venus smirked. "It's a surprise. You'll like it. You know, the longer you stay in your room, the more people believe Erek's refusal to talk about last night is proof the two of you hooked up."

"That's what they're talking about?" Kirby shouldn't be surprised. "No one cares I was manhandled and dragged to Loki's office in the middle of the night?"

"You did fuck the one person he thinks you're conspiring with, didn't you?" Ice Queen asked. "You poked Loki's ego. What did you expect him to do?"

"He doesn't realize you're conspiring with us instead. Get changed. Let's go." Venus pointed Kirby toward her bedroom.

Changed presumably meant into the same thing Ice Queen and Venus were wearing.

Kirby left the door open while she shed her jeans and yanked on the camo pants. She grew up sharing a dorm room with these women. They'd all seen each other already. "Give me a hint about what we're doing?" she called.

"Testing a theory," Ice Queen said.

Kirby shrugged a long-sleeved top on over her T-shirt, buttoned up, and grabbed her cap. "What kind of theory requires this?" The uniforms were usually reserved for semi-formal gatherings.

"The ceremonial kind," Venus replied.

The ceremonial kind of theory? That didn't make sense. Kirby rejoined them. "You've got me curious."

Ice Queen grabbed her hand and tugged her out of the room. "Good."

Kirby expected them to head for Ice Queen's Jeep in the parking lot, but instead they walked toward the trees surrounding the campus perimeter.

"Did you really break your hookup fast with a grunt? *That* grunt?" Venus handed her a pistol in a hip holster.

Even if last night's sex had only been that, the disdain in Venus's voice today would have made the escapade worth it. Kirby clipped the holster in place, and unsnapped the strap holding the weapon in. She withdrew the Desert Eagle .40. The magazine was full, and a round was chambered. "Is that what Erek's telling people?"

"He's not telling anyone anything. He's one of those guys who brags about every conquest, real or not, and he's refusing to talk about what happened after he left his ride home last night," Ice Queen said.

Min wasn't in it for the conquest. Erek knew keeping quiet would look a lot more real than bragging, plus not saying anything meant deniability if anyone asked why he was spreading rumors.

"Like you said, what better way to poke Loki's ego than by openly proving I don't care what he thinks?" Kirby holstered her gun again but kept the strap unsnapped. It was comforting to be carrying again. "Besides arming me, of course."

Venus flashed her a grin. "Thought you'd like that. It's yours. Happy belated birthday. How was he?"

No one would ever be able to compare notes on sex with Erek again, so it didn't matter what she said. "I'm not admitting anything, but if I were, really fucking incredible for a guy who has to brag about how good he is."

Ice Queen snorted a laugh. "No shit? Did you tell him that?"

They crossed the forest line, and the trees grew dense quickly as they continued. A gorgeous assortment of evergreens. "Not in so many words. The *Oh God, yeses* might have given me away."

"No wonder he's not talking. *No one* would believe he was capable of that." Venus led the way through a winding, barely-there path through the underbrush. The occasional snapped twig was the only indicator someone else had been through here recently.

They were a few hundred meters in, far enough that only trees were visible in any direction, when they reached a small clearing.

The soldier in full gear—including combat vest, cap, and firearms—who was tied to a tree made Kirby's gut lurch. Her reaction never showed. "Kinky. Which one of you is into sharing?" Besides her. If only the situation felt group-sex harmless.

"Ice Queen and I have a theory." Melon-head was here, as well as Cyclops. It was like a twisted version of *Nancy Drew meets the Hardy Boys*, if they solved mysteries by picking people off at three-hundred meters. "We're too focused on the details of a plan that, by Hel's own words, is supposed to be nearly foolproof."

"We think the death is more important than the details," Ice Queen said.

Melon-head jerked a thumb at the soldier. "This upstanding member of our infantry has volunteered to be our test sacrifice."

They were serious. Even the guy tied to the tree looked solemn, rather than afraid. Holy fuck, Kirby'd stepped into an honest-to-goddess cult.

Except she'd known that for years. Looking reality in the eye like this brought on a whole new level of awareness. Kirby couldn't let them just kill this guy. A year ago, Brit wouldn't have stopped them, but even she'd changed enough that fear no longer held her back. "You're just going to execute him?"

Cyclops frowned at her. "He's okay with it."

"All in her name." The soldier actually puffed out his chest when he said it.

Kirby didn't know his name; he was enough younger she'd never trained with him. Probably not even twenty-one. Old enough to die for Mistress Hel, but not to buy his own beer.

"Don't be all cliché squeamish about this," Venus said. "We're literally trained killers. You've executed how many random strangers on the streets, and this bothers you?"

As Kirby, she'd even looked Nobles in the eye and pulled the trigger. But Brit hated killing potentials as much as Kirby did, and neither of them had to do it anymore. "This is different."

"How?" Melon-head asked.

Everyone was staring at her with a combination of disbelief and irritation. Standing up for what she believed in was one thing, but being shot, and exposed as an imposter before she could solve the bigger issue, was stupid.

Brit was an incredible improviser, though, and an answer rushed to the tip of her tongue before Kirby had a chance to panic "Hel didn't train an entire army so we could bind our own to a tree, like a helpless fucking animal, when it came time to honor her name. This is lazy. Cowardly."

Ice Queen's frown deepened. *Please don't let this backfire.* "It's a fair point."

"Though you've got to wonder if some of her ex-partner's sadism rubbed off on her." Cyclops unsheathed his dagger and cut the soldier's bindings.

Something wasn't right. "How do you figure?" Kirby asked.

Melon-head winked. "Hunting him makes it seem like sport."

Oh fuck. "I wasn't—"

"Run, grunt," Cyclops growled in the soldier's ear.

Instead of sprinting into the forest, the soldier drew his gun.

Five weapons, including Kirby's new pistol, were trained on him in a heartbeat, but he didn't aim at the Nobles.

"I was promised glory for Hel. *For death.*" The soldier stuck the barrel in his mouth and pulled the trigger.

The abruptness of the gunshot and the resulting gore curdled everything inside Kirby, but Brit never let it show. What the fuck?

As his blood hit the dirt, the ground shook underneath their feet. It was a light tremor but enough to make them sway.

Melon-head and Ice Queen whooped, and Kirby's heart slammed against her ribs.

"It worked." Melon-head surveyed the carnage. "We're on the right path."

"So, we have to have everyone execute themselves?" Cyclops sounded skeptical.

Ice Queen toed the body. "More practical than the four of us trying to tie up every single one of them and shoot them." Her expression and tone embodied her name.

"What about those who refuse to participate?" Venus asked. "Valkyrie's not the only non-believer to come out of this place. The rest are just smarter about hiding it."

Smarter. Would Kirby have become like this, if Brit hadn't betrayed her? She'd like to think *no*, but she'd never considered an alternative before that day, in front of her judges.

Cyclops shrugged. "Kill your unwilling neighbor, then kill yourself."

The conversation, as cool and casual as if they were making dinner plans, sliced through Kirby. "You know that's a unique kind of psychology, right? That's not just pulling the trigger; it's turning on the people they were raised with. Turning a gun on themselves."

"Are you backing out on us, Kitten?" The way Venus studied her made Kirby uneasy. "Hel gave you yours, and now you don't want to share the glory? I'd hoped maybe you left the *holier than thou* attitude in your grave."

Melon-head screwed up his face and shook his head. "No, she's right. It is a mindset, and it's one even some believers will struggle with, especially if a friend is begging them not to pull the trigger."

"Because people are weak." Kirby wanted to vomit at the words. At how they tasted. How easy it was to fill her voice with disdain. Everyone on campus needing to die for Hel's resurrection just became far too tangible, and these people were willing to do anything to make it happen.

CHAPTER TWENTY-FIVE

Min crept through the forest, his attention focused on the environment, while cross chatter from his teammates echoed in his ear. Erek was a good soldier and a better strategist, and their plan was his.

"I bet she's insatiably domineering."

"No way. The control is all a show. She probably caved the minute he whipped his cock out."

"Bullshit. She never let him near her. He's going to be tied to the flagpole by tonight, for not denying everything."

Everyone wanted to talk about whether or not he'd fucked the campus's top sniper last night. His refusal to confirm or deny added fuel to the rumors, which was perfect for his purposes.

The game was Capture the Flag, and the winners got bragging rights. Around here, that was everything.

Wind whistled through the trees, rattling branches and adding a twisted sort of applause to the talk. Min wanted them talking about him. To him. He wanted it to look like they were more fascinated with gossiping about where his dick had been, than with hunting a flag.

While they talked, he would circle the perimeter pick off the other team one by one, take their flag, and rub their noses in the careless loss. The plan wouldn't work with everyone. That was the genius of it. Amy believed that Erek believed the world revolved around him, and she was the opposing team leader.

He came up behind the first soldier and hit him squarely between the shoulder blades with a paintball. The stealth kill meant the solder wasn't allowed to make a sound or indicate he'd died. He had to sit down and wait until the game was up.

"She reminds me of that Abenaki girl I hooked up with a few times, and I'm telling you, she's all rawr until you get her pants off. Then she's purring and begging."

Min moved on. Adrenaline raced through his veins. An intoxicating blend of tension and confidence. It choked his lungs and clouded his thoughts. The feeling was normal for Erek, but it was one of the sensations Min was most eager to be rid of.

Did Kirby live like this every day? From the things she'd told him when they were in London and she was struggling to make him understand her, she did. He hadn't gotten it at the time, regardless of how much he wanted to. Living as Erek, he didn't know how Kirby could see the world any other way.

"She was nuts, though. Wasn't she?"

"Oh yeah. Full on worshiped a goddess of fucking destruction. Swore she was coming back one day."

Min hit his next target in the side of the neck. The solder cringed—that had to sting—but didn't make a sound. Incredible discipline.

"How's that different from what the Nobles are up to?"

Min's thoughts froze for a heartbeat. He needed to let the chatter flow over him and get this done. He found the next target and landed another kill shot.

"You're serious? We've actually met Hel. Seen what she's capable of."

They really had no idea.

"No one's even seen this woman. She's been locked away for centuries. If she's even real."

They were believers, all right. *My god exists but yours is imaginary* was an ancient tale.

"And what if the bullshit about Hel coming back isn't real either?"

"The Nobles are proving it today."

What? Min picked off his next target. Only two left—Amy and the soldier guarding the flag—and Amy would find Min soon. He swallowed the urge to ask his team more about what they meant.

"Proving it how? Are we going to get back to the dorms and she'll be there?"

"You know Dustin? He volunteered to be their blood sacrifice."

That couldn't be good.

A gun pressed into his temple. "I'm firmly in the *she didn't let you touch her* court," Amy said softly.

Min smirked through the pain when she shot him in the side of the head. She wasn't supposed to do that at point-blank range, and it hurt like hell, but he never made a sound, though he had the right to cry out, since she'd made her presence known.

Another soft shot pinged behind him, and Amy dropped to the forest floor next to him without a sound, a dark scowl on her face.

Jakob stepped past both of them and exchanged thumbs up with Min, before continuing toward the enemy flag.

A moment later, his loud *whoop* rang through the forest.

"*Got it.*" His voice came over coms. He'd be on both channels now. Not that anyone from the other team was around to stop him.

"I can't believe you sacrificed your own glory for victory." Amy sounded both irritated and impressed.

Min stood and offered her a hand up. "It's always about the team, isn't it?" he asked.

She eyed him skeptically. "Yeah, but not to you."

A gunshot sounded in the distance. Not unusual around here, but this hadn't come from the direction of the shooting range. Min's memory stumbled back to L.A. in 1992. The riots. The last time Kirby died.

He didn't want to shove the memory aside. He needed to get to her, fuck the consequences.

The ground rolled beneath him in a strong enough quake to challenge his balance.

"That wasn't right." Amy shared his sentiment.

The magic in the shake was worse than she knew. It wasn't Hel; Min had never tasted this flavor of energy before. It was rotten earth, mixed with blood and destruction—the antithesis of everything Min represented.

Their commander called for everyone to fall in. The chatter continued as the company headed back to turn in their gear, but everyone else had moved on to other things. Min itched to investigate the gunshot. To know Kirby was safe.

The odds she'd been anywhere near the event were low, but so were the odds of a random carjacker choosing *Min's* car, and shooting the one person in it who could die from a gunshot.

With their guns, headsets, and everything else returned, the group moved toward the dorms. Some drifted off in the direction of the cafeteria or the library. They had free time now.

"Private Erek." Brit's voice stopped him in his tracks.

A symphony of *ooh*s and whistles sang out around him.

What was Kirby doing here? He was grateful she was alive, but to approach him on campus, in front of his entire company, was pushing a lot more boundaries than what they'd done last night.

He turned to face her, and saluted, as did everyone else. "Sergeant."

"With me. *Now*," she barked.

The constant background noise of tension that kept him moving cranked to full blast. "Yes, sir."

The whistles and cheers didn't start again until they were several meters away.

Kirby pulled him into a tucked away alcove in the library building. Erek assumed she wanted *Round Two*, but Min knew better. "You need to know what I heard during training," he said.

"You can't stay here." Her voice was tight, each word clipped.

What? "This is about the earthquake, isn't it? The gunshot?"

She nodded. Her gaze darted in every direction, never focusing on one point for too long, and rarely landing on him. "It's not safe for any grunt here. And if you're their next target, you'll blow both our covers. You need to go back. Tell the others." As she related the story of what had happened in the woods, with the other Nobles, Min's concern grew.

"That falls in line with what I heard." He gave her a brief recap of the chatter during his mission.

Her eyes widened in understanding. *"Fuck."* She scrubbed her face, exhaling through her fingers. "Malsumis. The one they sell the merchandise for, in the souvenir shops. The locals believe she was imprisoned by other gods, and that blood spilled on this soil under the right circumstances will free her."

"They're not going to bring Hel back."

"But they think they are. Instead, she's set them up with someone far more vindictive."

More vindictive than Hel was a terrifying thought. Understanding spread through Min. "Her plan is foolproof, because it only requires death."

"Not *only*," Kirby said. "It has to be blood spilled by a true believer. It's why Blossom and Fumbles… Dahlia, other Nobles aren't here. They didn't believe. They were sent on useless errands, to keep them from interfering in what's about to happen."

The people Min had sent Starkad after, when he first became Erek. "We're leaving. Now."

"No." Kirby's tone was hard. "*You're* leaving. I'm making a pact with the lesser of two-evils."

"What does that mean? No. We both go back. We regroup. We plan next steps as a team." Min wouldn't leave her, and Erek refused to let her execute a poorly thought out plan.

Her smile didn't reach her eyes. She stood on her toes and brushed her lips over his. Desperation and sorrow flooded through the soft connection. "If you don't hear from me in two hours, then you can come after me."

"What? *No.* I—"

"Tell Starkad to let Brit go. I'll see you soon. *Ástvinur.*"

Min stumbled at being back in his own body, and a void sat in his mind where Erek used to be. The campus vanished, and he was back in Aeval's palace.

"*Damn it, Kirby,*" he roared in the empty entryway. What had she done?

CHAPTER TWENTY-SIX

Kirby ached at having to send Min away. Finally seeing his face again, even for a heartbeat, was beautiful agony. Then removing the one person from her side who had her back...

She could stroll across campus again, but after the scene she'd made with Erek, that would draw more attention than she cared for. She preferred if people thought she and he were still here, hiding in the stacks.

Kirby closed her eyes and summoned a prayer. "Loki, I know you're keeping an eye on me," she muttered. She might not worship this god, but she desperately needed him to hear her, and that should be enough. "I need you here." She hated how much she meant those words.

Nothing.

And then a new heat at her back. "You're not *that* important," Loki whispered in her ear.

"You came, didn't you?" Kirby wasn't the only one who couldn't afford to turn down allies. She'd had her doubts about Loki's motivations, but the fact that he showed up so quickly squelched some of her noisier concerns.

She needed to stay on campus as Brit. But she also needed to communicate with Starkad. To share information and build a strategy. Going through Loki was the best way to ensure that, if someone had to know what she was up to, it was someone with as much to lose as her.

"Let's go somewhere more private and talk," Loki said, and then they were in his office. "Now then, you were saying?"

"You were right. About who I am, about why I'm here, and about my needing your help." She mentally rolled her eyes.

Loki strolled to the other side of his desk and sat. His posture was calm. Confident. "*Fuck*, it must hurt to admit that."

A bit, yeah. "It kills me dead. If you were hoping for more, this is the closest I get to groveling."

"What happens if I lied?"

"*If?*" Kirby barked a laugh. "However, you do want this. For this place to stay standing. To use an entire private army to shield you from a single girl. To talk to Davyn." She didn't hesitate to dangle the last offer, since Davyn wanted the same thing. They were big boys; they could choose to write their own mutually assured destruction. "You don't get any of that if you fuck me over too soon."

"I don't get any of that right now, even if I work with you. Easy enough for you to make offers when you get paid up front and I have to wait."

This time she didn't hide the eyeroll. "Did you feel the earthquake less than an hour ago? Time is critical."

"I know." Loki sighed. "Hel was never talking about Brit when she said one of her followers would return. She meant you. *Kirby*."

Bullshit. "She never made me feel like a part of anything here. Why would I come back?" Then again, she's isolated Brit pretty completely, too. How many Nobles felt that way, but never let it show?

"It didn't matter if you returned to serve her. It was pretty much guaranteed that you'd return. But she knew who you were when you arrived—we all did. And I don't mean the Valkyrie bit. You weren't a killer. She pushed with everything, to make you hate the outside world. To bend you to her will. To break you in her favor."

Bile rose in Kirby's throat. She'd suspected as much, especially with Brit's memories backing up the theory, but hearing someone say it outright... He could be lying, but this was something that felt real. "That's fucked up." She kept the emotion from her voice. Thank Brit for that.

"She's arranged to have hundreds of people who worship her killed, so she can live again. You expected reasonable?"

The gods rarely were. "Great. We've both groveled. I'll tell you everything I know, if you give me an outside line to Starkad and let me bring him in for backup."

"This goes back to what I said about paying up front. I don't like having you here. I don't like having him anywhere."

243

"I can leave right now and let you deal with the death. With Hel." Kirby was bluffing, and it wasn't a good bluff. She'd do everything in her power, to keep a goddess of destruction—one the other gods were scared of enough to lock away—from being released.

Loki smirked. "If you were willing to do that, you wouldn't be here in the first place. Tell me what you know, and I'll decide if the threat is worth the risk of bringing in backup."

Negotiating was an option, but there were some things Kirby wasn't willing to bend on. "You're not a tactician. You're a salesman and an administrator, and if you had the skills these soldiers do, you wouldn't need them. I say who my backup is."

"Don't insult me while you want favors from me. I don't want to do this without your help, but I will. But I can evict you from the campus right now, and you won't be back." Was *he* bluffing? There was only so far she was willing to push. "I'm doing this to save my own neck, which won't happen if you stick my head on the chopping block for someone else."

She clenched her jaw. "Fine. The Nobles have figured out there *is* no ritual to follow, beyond a believer spilling blood." She wasn't giving up everything, though. There was no way to know how he'd react to the news about a different goddess being released. "And as you waste my fucking time, proving your dick is bigger, they're figuring out the best way to kill as many people as possible, simultaneously, with a lot of bloodshed. We need to isolate them, and if they figure out we're coming for them, it won't be easy. I'm not doing that without backup I trust."

"Correct me if I'm wrong, but you've spent the last few years hunting Nobles."

Holy fuck. Did he understand the concept of *time is of the essence?* How long was he going to drag this out?

"I wasn't alone. I only went after two at a time," Kirby said. "And they didn't know I was going to be there. There are a dozen Noble teams on campus, and once they get wind someone is picking them off on their home turf..."

Loki's drawn-out sigh made it seem like he was about to make the biggest sacrifice of his life. "All right. Bring in—"

The sound of the doorframe splintering filled the room. Loki's office door was kicked open. Kirby reached for her gun as she spun, but the person pressing a barrel to the back of her head was faster.

CHAPTER TWENTY-SEVEN

"Damn it, Kirby."

When Gwydion heard Min's roar echo through the palace, his blood turned to ice and he broke into a sprint, racing toward the shout. He found Min in the foyer, looking like the embodiment of fury and anguish.

"What happened?" Gwydion demanded.

"She sent me back alone. Where are the others? We're going back now."

Gwydion agreed with the sentiment, but not with the logistics. As much as it devoured him to argue, he had to. "If Kirby made the decision, she had a reason for it. Did she tell you anything?"

"Where are the others? This is the last time I'll repeat myself, so they'd better be here when I explain." Magic splashed white in stark contrast over Min's dark skin.

Gwydion rarely saw this side of him, and it was terrifying. Min believed Kirby was in extreme danger. "I just dropped them off to meet up with a friend—associate?—of Starkad's." Which should be good news. Davyn couldn't be fond of Loki, and more muscle wouldn't hurt. "Let's go."

He opened a doorway and stepped through. Min would follow, and there was no time to waste.

They arrived in a small town, in an alley behind a row of buildings that were barely a century old. The ambient magic crawled through Gwydion like a million tiny pinpricks. Something was wrong with the earth here. The trees and other plants were tainted with something foul.

"How far are we from campus?" Min stepped past him.

Gwydion matched his stride. "About two hours."

"Not close enough. Where are they?"

It wasn't a big enough town that finding Brit and Starkad would be difficult, but every wasted second without Kirby or answers was agony to Gwydion. If the air felt like this and she was closer to the source, he wanted to take her as far away as possible.

They rounded one corner, and then another, to get to the main street. Less than a block away, Starkad stood in front of Brit, staring down Davyn.

Wonderful.

"I take it that's Starkad's friend." Min kept walking.

"What gave it away?" Gwydion had been on Davyn's side of that staring match more than a few times. He and Min approached quickly. "Stand down, boys. More important things are happening."

Davyn growled. That was supposed to be impressive? "She lied to me. Tried to kill my ward. Has killed dozens of others."

Starkad was protecting Brit? That was new.

"One—I've never met you before. Not face to face." Brit's voice shook, but there was no hesitation in her retort. "Two—I never intended to kill her. The plan was always to execute my partner and walk away. Your girl was never in danger from me. And three, it hasn't been dozens, but it has been more than I care to admit."

"Where's Kirby?" Starkad's gaze never left Davyn, but he was talking to Min.

"Still inside. Hence the *more important things*."

Davyn broke the staring match first, to glance at Min. "Inside where?"

"TOM. You didn't talk to her"—Starkad jerked his thumb toward Brit—"you spoke with Kirby, dressed as her. And if she's in danger, you've become my lowest priority."

"Let me rip the sniper's throat out, and I'll help you find the Valkyrie," Davyn said.

Charming. "This isn't a negotiation. I can put you in a cell in the fae realm in a blink. Brit didn't kill your girl or even injure her." And Gwydion was still a little irritated that Azzie had pulled a knife on him. "Stand down and either walk away or help us."

Davyn's nose grew longer, becoming more of a snout, and his teeth grew as well.

Gwydion summoned a doorway next to himself and rattled the earth under Davyn's feet to nudge the bear toward the gate. The magic didn't come as easily as it should have been, thanks to whatever lingered here, but Gwydion hid his strain.

Davyn's bear-like features receded. "I reserve the right to kill the sniper later."

"No, you don't." Min's voice was stone.

Brit stepped forward. "Kirby?"

Gwydion didn't suspect anyone was in the mood to *go sit someplace and talk.*

Min still wore the furious mask. "She sent me back. Told me she was going to make a deal with the lesser of two evils, and that if we didn't hear from her in two hours, things didn't go as planned."

Fuck the two-hour waiting period. "Let's go."

"Did she send you with other information?" Starkad asked.

"We can't go in there without a plan," Brit added. "Kirby knows what she's doing, and stepping on her toes without coordination is likely to be more dangerous than the alternative."

Their logic sucked. They were right, but that didn't mean Gwydion liked it.

Min managed the most punctuated sigh in history. "They think they're trying to bring Hel back, but their actions won't. There's another goddess imprisoned here. Malsumis. Blood spilled by believers will free her."

"Shit. Was that the quake earlier?" Davyn's hostility vanished.

"Testing a theory about bloodshed." Min nodded.

Davyn paced. "We may be too late."

"How much time do we have left?" Starkad looked at Min.

"Hour forty-five."

Min didn't talk like that. Were the side effects of being someone else lingering?

"Not a lot of time, but enough for a plan and a debrief." Brit looked at Gwydion. "Take us to the castle, in case she's already there."

Best suggestion Gwydion had heard so far. He summoned a portal.

"You don't understand," Davyn said. "Malsumis is Azzie's father—well, other mother, but it's a god thing." He must mean both the impregnation by a goddess, and the ability to do so while imprisoned. "Carrying a goddess's baby had side effects for Azzie's mother. Over and over, she saw visions of the world burning, if Malsumis was freed."

This was so very bad. Even before Malsumis vanished, she'd been a vicious god, bordering on insanity, and hungry for vengeance. She'd sworn to inflict the same fate on the modern occupants of this land that they had on her people.

Which was a sentiment Gwydion understood. He'd gone to war for less. But he wouldn't do it again, and the loss of hundreds or millions of lives wouldn't bring anyone back.

Chapter Twenty-Eight

Kirby reappeared in the woods outside of campus, Loki by her side. At least he hadn't left her to deal with the intruders alone.

"Were they Nobles?" she asked.

He nodded. "Drop the mask. I want to look *you* in the eye for this. You're not nearly as good a liar as Brit is."

Charming. Kirby didn't have a reason to hide anymore. That game was up. She focused on sending Brit's *ka* on its way in a far less jarring manner than Min's safeword would. Her joints felt as if they were expanding and relaxing at the same time, like undoing a too-tight pair of jeans. Speaking of, her pants were too loose now. The nice thing about the BDU's, though, was that they were baggy enough that the fit didn't matter anywhere but the waist.

"Don't suppose you'll let me borrow your belt." Kirby's voice sounded odd to her own ears. It was the familiar timbre she'd heard across the centuries, but it wasn't right. She hitched up the waist of her pants as they slipped down her hips.

Loki did a great job of sighing and groaning, exaggerating the inconvenience, as he stripped off his belt and handed it to her. Loose slacks were a tiny thing, but they'd ruin a good game of cat and mouse if they fell off at the wrong time.

Kirby wanted to believe she and Loki were the cats, but they weren't. Not today.

"Where's Starkad? I'll take you to him," Loki said.

Aeval had given them a lot of freedom to come and go from her home and realm, but bringing in an uninvited god—one most gods didn't get along with—was rude and possibly dangerous. If Loki was even capable of entering without her permission.

"We have to call him"—it was powerful magic to let phones still work there—"Or you have to let me go back to the faery realm alone, to get him."

"That explains why I couldn't find you. You're staying by my side, and we're not doing a long, drug out negotiation again."

A suppressed gunshot sounded and a bullet bit into Kirby's arm. Pain screamed through her. The forest vanished, and a different part of campus appeared around them. She clenched her fists, digging her nails into her palms, to ignore the agony spreading from her fresh wound. It took her several seconds of focus, to move past the pain.

Bullets weren't supposed to hurt her. Especially not this much. "See why we need to work together? Take me to the other side of the world so we can make a plan and I can call Starkad." *Fucking fuck,* this hurt. Stars danced in front of her eyes. "Or at least take us into town."

"I've been trying. Something is keeping me here."

How wonderfully not wonderful. "I'm going back for Starkad. Don't move. We'll return for you."

"Don't you dare." Loki grabbed her bad arm.

She bit the inside of her cheek until she tasted copper, to keep from screaming, and activated her one-time key home. Nothing happened. Had she wasted her chance by sending Min back? No. Aeval had assured her this wouldn't be an issue.

"Something wrong?" Loki let go of her.

Everything was wrong. "Lucky you, we're going to do this by ourselves, just like you wanted." They had an hour and a half until the others returned, but if she and Loki couldn't get out by magical means, Gwydion probably couldn't get in. This was just like what Aeval experienced in the warehouse. "Are you doing this?"

Loki raised his brows. "Yes. I like being hunted by Nobles who want me dead as much as I do them."

Was he protesting too much? It didn't matter, if she had no alternative but to work with him until her backup arrived. "Don't suppose you can get us into the armory." Every second out in the open, especially with no plans and only one magazine for her pistol, was more dangerous than the last.

"The instant we show up there, others will know."

Kirby was aware. "Then we'd better move fast."

If she had any idea at all which soldiers weren't pro-Hel, which Campus Police would rather live than be sacrifices, she'd go on a recruiting spree. Having lots of guns would have to do.

They made two stops in the armory—one for weapons and one for ammo—and Kirby shoved as much as would fit into a single duffel bag.

Loki teleported them to a new location, this one with a wall of rocks that acted as a natural barrier. At least he had some sense of tactics. "You're going to carry those with you? You can barely lift your arm. What's going on with that, by the way?"

Her arm was actually feeling better. The initial shock had faded, and she could move the limb with only minor complaint. "I'm going to carry a reasonable amount and stow the rest here." The Nobles were already armed, so it didn't matter if they found the stash. Kirby would prefer they didn't, but it wasn't game-breaking.

"I need to think." She slid to the ground with her back to a large rock, and shoved panic aside. If she and Loki stayed on the defensive, they'd never accomplish anything. Putting the urge to run on hold left room for the rest of reality to sink in. It had only been a couple of weeks since she became Brit, but with that extra set of thoughts gone, there was an empty pit inside.

Brit knew how Ice Queen and Melon-head thought. She'd be able to guess their next steps. The best Kirby could do was figure out the mostly likely approach Starkad would take to get onto campus, if he came in on foot. Useful when the time came, but not nearly as much so if she and Loki didn't accomplish anything before backup arrived.

An hour and fifteen minutes left, before she told Min to come for her if she hadn't returned. And she had no doubt Starkad would be here. Enough time to find at least a couple of Nobles. But was it? She was intimately familiar with the training here, but they'd realize that. They wouldn't follow standard steps. Unless they did.

Stop. She could follow the logic around all day, and the only thing that would do was paralyze her with indecision. It didn't matter that she'd only ever hunted Nobles in pairs, because that was all they were now. She could only pursue one pair at a time, and that was how they'd be looking for her. She could do this, as long as she picked a starting point.

"*Fuck.*" Loki's exclamation jarred her. He hovered a hand over her injured arm. "You're not healing."

She craned her neck to view the wound, as she tried to move her arm. The limb didn't respond. A red stain mixed with black spread out from the hole. She tugged up the cuff of her sleeve, and her arm was dead weight, unmoving and numb. Dark lines ran under her skin, like inky poisoned veins.

"I can still shoot with my left hand." It wasn't a solution, but it was the only thought Kirby could process. That was a lot more promising than, *What the fuck is wrong with my arm?*

Loki grimaced. "Not if this spreads."

She hovered her hand over the wound and focused on her healing magic. The pleasantly warm salve flowed over her. Sparks flared from the bullet hole, and she swallowed a yelp. What was the point in having super-healing Valkyrie powers if she couldn't use them?

CHAPTER TWENTY-NINE

Kirby wasn't going to surrender just because some mysterious magic was gnawing away at her arm. She pointed to the duffel bag. "Grab whatever you're comfortable with, along with a few extra magazines of ammo."

"I'm good. Which direction are we heading? Or are we bringing them to us?" Loki said.

"Are you too nice a guy to shoot someone?" Given he'd had a hand in raising an entire school of gunmen, that was hard to believe.

Loki shrugged. "Sure. Let's go with that."

Ah. "You're not skilled enough."

"I didn't say that. Plan?"

He didn't deny her assumption, either. This might be better, as Kirby didn't want him killing anyone unless he had to. "Can you disable someone from a distance?"

Loki summoned a baseball-sized globe of lightning, let it hover a few centimeters over his hand, and tossed it at a nearby tree. It struck the trunk and left an impressive scorched crater in its wake.

It also made a significant amount of noise. "Way to let them know we're here." Kirby didn't bother to hide her irritation. "Can you do that without killing someone?"

"I don't understand the question." He looked at her as if she were speaking a foreign language.

Gods, the next hour was going to take forever to pass. "I don't want you to kill anyone. Not until we have more information."

"I'm sorry—who put you in charge?"

"We do it my way, or you find them on your own."

Loki rolled his eyes. "Let's not do this bluffing bullshit again. If I can touch them, I can put them to sleep. I promise not to kill anyone unless I have to, *Team Leader Valkyrie*."

His disdain and the nickname clawed under her skin and gnawed at her thoughts. "Great. Follow me. Be quiet." There was no way she'd tell him her entire plan. They were looking for Nobles, true. Trying to find the other snipers before they found Kirby. But she was also working her way toward the outer perimeter of the campus. Assuming Gwydion couldn't magically get in any more than Loki could get out, she wanted to be at the most likely place for Starkad to arrive on foot.

If the Nobles knew teleporting in and out was disabled, and if they expected Starkad, they'd have someone positioned near Kirby's destination. Whether they were there or not didn't matter—Kirby and Loki would disable one or two teams from the entrance point as readily as she'd hide and wait for backup.

She and Loki picked their way through the trees, with Kirby in the lead. She hated having him at her back. *Lesser of two evils* wasn't a comforting reason to take her eyes off the god. But it was easier to travel single file, and she only trusted her own sight on the area.

Brit should be completely gone from her head, but impressions lingered. It was different than actually being Brit. More like if Kirby had watched a movie of Brit's life and could summon certain memories and emotions.

It made it easier to understand the egos of the people hunting them.

The underbrush was disturbed here. A handful of broken twigs and crumbled leaves were packed into the dirt. She held up her good hand, motioning for Loki to stop. Normally, she'd clench her fist, but that was hard to do while holding a pistol. She stepped behind a nearby tree, and Loki followed.

The wind swirled around them, creating eddies of leaves in pockets of trees. Kirby strained her ears, searching for anything out of place.

Nothing. But people had been through here recently. They might have left someone on watch. She had to take a chance. *Please let Loki understand my hand gestures*. She pointed two fingers toward his eyes, then gestured around them, indicating he needed to watch the area.

If she were doing this, she'd be in a tree and her spotter would be in a different one, near enough that any clicks sent over the radio could be interpreted as directions.

But they knew she was out here, and they weren't going to do what she would.

Kirby braced herself and sprinted across the short clearing, to the next tree. A suppressed bullet bit the dirt in front of her, and then another at her heels, as she ducked behind another trunk.

Loki was gone.

Based on where the shots came from, the spotter was most likely a few trees over from Kirby and actively searching for her. Kirby stayed hidden, listening for a breath or the *crack* of a twig she'd never hear. They'd pursue her. She didn't need to go to them.

A soft *thunk* reached her ears, and she whirled to see Loki standing next to Crazy Eight, who was unconscious on the forest floor.

Loki pressed his mouth to her ear, and unpleasantness crawled over her skin. "I'm locking them under the cafeteria. Used to be a boiler room, now it's not," he whispered.

She nodded. Loki vanished with Crazy Eight, and returned alone seconds later.

The Nobles would have communication, but they'd likely maintain radio silence so she didn't hear them talking in the middle of the forest. With each team she and Loki removed from the equation, there was a larger chance someone would notice people were disappearing.

Kirby's heart slammed against her ribs as they moved forward again. An ache ran from her shoulder into her neck, making her wish she could pop something, to alleviate the growing discomfort. She didn't want to look at her arm but couldn't help it. The infection was growing. The flesh nearest the hole had blackened and deteriorated.

Could TOM do this to any immortal? Maybe they had special ammo loaded in their guns just for her, but that was highly impractical. What were Starkad and the others walking into? Her fear grew. Was this what Min felt every time he watched her die? What the others felt?

She swallowed her terror as best she could.

A short while later, she and Loki came up behind another team. Actually saw their backs, before the team saw Kirby. With a few blinks, Loki had incapacitated them and removed them from the scene.

Having him here was nicer than she'd expected.

Her pulse roared in her ears, partly from adrenaline but mostly from the growing pain in her arm. The numbness had left her, and her right side felt like it was on fire. Her breath came in short gasps, as she struggled to draw in air.

"Sit. Rest," Loki whispered in her ear.

Kirby didn't want to. She didn't have a choice. She sank to the ground, and focused on slowing her heart and ignoring the pain.

"Valkyrie." Ice Queen's voice startled her. *Fuck.* "I wonder who got a shot off at you. Doesn't matter, because I get to finish the job." The volume of her tone was normal, so she wasn't trying to alert anyone besides Venus to where she was. And Venus was around somewhere.

"Gloating? Really?" Kirby was surprised she kept her voice steady. "You could have shot me, and you want to talk?"

"Yeah, I want to talk. Because, for you, there's a life after this one, and I want you to die knowing you failed to destroy us. You were the best of us and you threw it all away. We were your brothers and sisters, and you gave us up for thousand-year-old dick?"

A school full of Alphas with egos. Exactly the way Hel wanted it. Kirby could either be amused or sob. "You were never anything to me."

"That's on you. You've got so much fucking ego, you couldn't even hide who you were when you came back. Brit would never have made the stupid mistakes you did. Would never have given herself to a grimy grunt. Would never have trusted us with—" Ice Queen dropped to the ground when Loki appeared behind her.

"Got them both," he said. "Be right back."

Kirby slumped against the tree again. That was three teams down, but more were still out there. Melon-head and Cyclops were the biggest threat, but definitely not the only one.

She needed to stand. To survey the area. It didn't matter how deep she dug; her reserves were almost depleted. Was she going to die out here?

The thought knocked her off-balance. She'd spent the last six years wondering if she wanted to die, and now that she was staring the prospect in the face, it terrified her. She wasn't ready to go.

She might not have a say in the matter.

CHAPTER THIRTY

Min had never watched a clock more closely in his existence. At fifteen minutes before *Time's Up*, Starkad had Gwydion open a portal. They'd arrive in the library, not far from where Kirby had been when she sent Min back. According to Brit, that was their best bet for minimal disturbance.

Except that Gwydion's magic didn't work.

Min's tension cranked a bit higher, as Aeval joined them to see what she could do.

After a few agonizing seconds of focus and a series of shimmers that blinked into view before vanishing again, she shook her head. "There's magic around that location that's keeping me from acting."

"We could have stayed where we were and driven, and we'd nearly be there by now." Davyn had protested the bulk of the options suggested during planning.

Min was nearly back to his own mind frame, but it was tempting to deck the large man, just to shut him up. Davyn was an amplified version of everything aggravating about Starkad. The asshole needed to get laid. "Work your way out," Min said.

Starkad nodded. "New spot, outside of campus." He showed Gwydion where on the map. "Start here and push in until you can't get through, then step back."

More time ticked away. More minutes wasted that Kirby was alone. Min wouldn't be so concerned if they'd heard from her.

"This is it." Gwydion's statement was carried on an odd mixture of relief and apprehension.

"I don't like going in blind," Davyn said.

"We're not blind. Not completely." Starkad's reply was less than reassuring. "Kirby will be near this point if she can be. If we don't find her, things are bad."

Davyn growled. He made a far more excessive use of the threatening sound than Starkad ever had. "Sounds pretty fucking blind to me."

Brit stepped up to the shimmering portal. "See you on the other side." And she was gone.

Starkad followed on her heels. He'd hesitated when it came time to decide if the group was going alone or in pairs, but Min's message from Kirby was enough to sway him to give Brit a chance.

Everyone else joined them, and Min stepped into a patch of dense forest.

"Gwydion with Min. Head southeast, and circle back to the original location. Davyn, with me. We'll go southwest." Starkad pointed at each of them. "Brit, due south. Good luck."

The assignments made sense—Gwydion and Davyn weren't familiar with the campus layout, but the group needed as many vectors as possible to do this.

The three teams fanned out, vanishing into the trees. Seconds crawled away, feeling like eons, as Min and Gwydion crept through foliage.

Something caught his attention up ahead. *Kirby*. Except she was down. Was she bait? Already caught and waiting? No, she wouldn't allow that.

Not that Min cared if it was a trap. He and Gwydion sprinted toward her. Fear gripped Min as they drew close and he made out details. She was pale, and her arm looked desiccated. He holstered his gun.

As soon as Gwydion gave the *all clear*, Min was going to scoop her up and carry her out of here, regardless of her protests.

Gwydion knelt at her side.

A movement flashed next to Min, and he had his gun out in a heartbeat, trained on the new arrival. Apparently more of Erek lingered in Min's veins than he'd realized.

Loki held up his hands, palms out.

"He's with me," Kirby croaked.

It wasn't enough for Min to drop his guard.

Gwydion poked at Kirby's arm, and his frown deepened.

"Am I gonna live, doc?" Her laugh was weak.

The question sliced like a blade through Min's chest. She'd asked the same thing in her last life, after protecting a building from being destroyed by a stray CRUZ missile. She sounded so much worse now.

"I don't know what to do with this."
Gwydion's despair was tangible.

Min holstered his gun and knelt next to her.
His instinct was to carry her away, but a different
compulsion raced inside. He brushed a hand over the
wound without making contact.

She squirmed and whimpered, but some of
the rot receded.

"It's killing you," Loki said.

Kirby glared at him. "No shit."

"No, I mean… *Fuck*, you're dense, for
someone who was created to be a bringer of death."

"I understand," Min said. He was life. The
magic infesting her was his opposite. He'd weakened
Hel when they fought her, and he should be able to
do the same to the disease crawling through Kirby.
"This is probably going to hurt. Tremendously."

"I won't scream. We can't afford it." Each
retort from Kirby sounded like it took more effort
than the last.

Min ripped the strap from his holster as if it
were paper, and held it in front of her mouth. "Bite
down. Hold onto Gwydion."

Gwydion grasped Kirby's hand, and Loki
turned away, sweeping his gaze over their
surroundings.

Min glided his palm millimeters from
Kirby's arm and focused on the wound. He could feel
the decay woven through her. He plucked at a tiny
strand, and she squirmed. He had to ignore her
discomfort, to do this. He summoned the same
emotions he felt when he found her fighting Hel. The

love. The rage. The need to see Kirby whole and alive.

The more magical pieces he tugged, the more her whimpers sounded like grunts.

Noises that would be enticing under other circumstances squeezed despair through him now. He dove deeper into the injury, replacing death with life. Burning away infection with passion.

Kirby had stopped moving, and her muffled screams devoured him.

Min kept going, pushing the limits of his magic and patience, exertion prickling his skin, until the last of the death in Kirby's arm burned away.

She went limp with a sigh.

Min withdrew from the semi-meditative state. Gwydion checked her pulse. Color was returning to her skin, and her breath came evenly.

Her eyelids fluttered open, and she focused on Min as she spat out the bit. "Thank you." The strength was returning quickly to her voice. The wound in her arm closed rapidly, until the only remnant was the hole in her shirt.

Min wanted to kiss her with relief. Embrace her. Take her as far from this place as possible. He understood why he couldn't—why she'd never forgive him if he forced that on her—so he settled for handing her an earpiece.

She fitted the device in place while she stood. "Someone talk to me."

Starkad's laugh of relief came over the radio. "You're alive."

"Duh." There wasn't as much sass in the retort as she probably intended.

"Locations." Brit reeled off a series of coordinates not attached to people's names.

Min muted his earpiece long enough to murmur, "There aren't that many of us here."

"I know." Kirby said.

Because she and Brit had been a team once. *The* team.

"Don't kill anyone." Kirby was on the radio again. "Restrain them, call in a location, and Loki will come for them."

"Loki? Where is he?" That was Davyn.

Kirby rolled her eyes and mouthed, *why is he here?*

In the interest of brevity, Min shrugged.

Kirby looked fully recovered.

A new final destination was conveyed—the cafeteria where Loki had imprisoned all the Nobles.

"I can't get the two of you to leave me, can I?" Kirby asked.

"Not for a long time." Min knew Gwydion shared the sentiment.

Loki made a gagging sound. "I'm going to do a little pop and run in random places. See if I can catch anyone off guard."

As the groups worked their way toward the rendezvous point, one capture after another was called in.

"That's almost everyone," Kirby said softly. "Only Cyclops and Melon-head are left."

A foreign sensation flooded Min, and instinct kicked in. He shoved Kirby behind a tree, covering her body with his, as a bullet bit into the ground next to her.

268

Gwydion took cover as well.

"Valkyrie, is that you?" Cyclops's call echoed through the trees. "It's been too long."

"*Gods*, these people are fucking cliché." Kirby met Min's gaze. "Right side, six meters up. I'll take the other one."

He processed the request on instinct, watching for her signal before stepping out from behind the tree.

Kirby mirrored his movement, and they fired in unison.

The sound of leaves crunching from two different directions reached them, as the bodies hit the ground.

The ground rumbled under Min's feet, obliterating his feeling of victory.

"What did you do?" Davyn demanded.

Min was tired of being reprimanded by a nearly wild animal. "We had to kill them. We didn't have a choice."

"Are you fucking insane? I thought you understood," Davyn shouted.

So much for discretion. The Nobles might be taken care of, but soldiers still roamed the campus.

"I thought..." Kirby faltered. "Believers, spilling blood. We're not believers."

"Believers' blood, being spilled," Davyn said.

Shit. Min's rage and terror were back, potent and cloying.

"Where's Loki?" Starkad demanded.

Brit came on. "He took the pair I snagged—"

"He's going to kill them. Cafeteria *now*." Min was already running.

CHAPTER THIRTY-ONE

Kirby didn't have time for running. Her wings appeared without effort, and her feet left the ground as she flew in the straightest path possible toward her destination.

Gwydion was by her side. There was no time to wait for anyone who couldn't keep up.

A low roar echoed around them, as if the earth was protesting. They reached their target first, and she was sprinting as she made contact with the pavement. Down the rear stairs of the building, to a concrete hallway that ran under the cafeteria. The ground rolled gently under her feet. They couldn't be too late.

A steel door stood in their way, as Loki had promised.

She and Gwydion couldn't break through.

The walls rattled around them.

One by one, the others arrived. A happy reunion would have been nice. It would wait.

"Cracks are growing underneath us," Gwydion said. "I can feel roots peeking through."

Could they speed up that process? Kirby looked at Davyn. "Brute force?"

His grin morphed into something terrifying, as he shifted into a bear.

Kirby and the others stepped back, as Gwydion summoned the trees. Gaps spread through the foundation and the walls surrounding the door.

Davyn plowed into the solid barricade once, and then again. With his third full-body slam, the door fell to the floor.

Loki stood in the middle of the room on the other side, a dozen bodies at his feet and blood pooling on the concrete around him.

"Fuck, you're an idiot." What else was there to say? The earth shook so hard it was difficult to remain upright. "They're the key—their blood. We had it wrong."

Loki's eyes were wide. Kirby'd never seen him afraid before. "You didn't tell me. This isn't Hel."

It didn't matter. He'd unleashed destruction on the world.

"He's here," Loki said.

He?

Kirby would sift through that later. A twisted and grotesque malevolence clawed over her, until all she saw in her mind was blackness. This being, whatever it was, was going to bring the campus down around people. So many lives would be lost.

Kirby didn't want hundreds to die. Desperation flooded her veins, and she reached

272

inside, grasping for any solution. Potent energy burst free from a dam in her mind, rushing from every pore.

She had to save people. As the power continued to flow from her, she swore she could see the path of the invisible shell that flooded the campus and encased every person in a shield.

Kirby held onto the thought. It might not be real, but she needed it to be.

It felt like an eternity, before the ground stopped shaking.

"He's gone."

The words were in her head. Was that Loki? She was so tired.

Consciousness seeped away, no matter how hard she struggled to hold onto it.

****

"Yes, you're going to live."

Gwydion's voice made Kirby smile as she woke up. She was weary, but as she tentatively tested various limbs and joints, nothing hurt. She risked opening her eyes. The lighting was dim, and the bed soft. Familiar scents enveloped her. She was home. *Actual* home, in her bedroom. Where she and Starkad lived. They hadn't been back since... everything.

Six months felt like so long ago. A wave of emotion choked her throat and welled up in her eyes.

"Hey." Gwydion brushed a thumb over her cheek, smearing a tear. "Does something hurt?"

"No. Yes. Nothing physical." With a few deep breaths, she let the wash flow through and from her. "What happened? To the campus? To Loki? With Malsumis? Me?"

"My official diagnosis is you're suffering from dick deficiency. Not nearly enough of it in the last few weeks."

Kirby laughed. Yup, things were at least a little right in the world. "If I was in someone else's body and I hooked up with a cocky grunt named Erek, is that cheating?" she teased.

"For him or you? Serious answer—you did that shield thing of yours, like in Kuwait, but it covered the whole campus. You've been asleep for more than twenty-four hours."

Memories rushed back. Her desire to keep people from dying. The power she'd pushed from herself. The shield did take a lot out of her. "What about everyone else?"

"Several of the buildings collapsed. You probably saved everyone inside them."

"*Probably?*"

"There were no bodies. None. Starkad and Davyn swept every place they could get into. They didn't see or smell anyone but us on the entire campus. We believe Gluskab took the TOM residents when he left."

"The brother?" Malsumis' twin.

Gwydion sighed, and for an instant, his true age showed in the lines on his face and the loss in his gaze. His smile forced the look away but didn't reach his eyes. "According to Loki—so take this with a grain of salt—Gluskab was grief stricken and driven to madness when his sister was imprisoned. So he made a deal with Hel, to sleep until brother and sister were strong enough to be released. He insists he would have told you, if you'd bothered to let him know what you were really up to."

Right. "And now that he's out, he's going for his sister?" There were two more pissed off gods about to be running free. Yay. "What do we do?"

"Same thing we do every night—" Gwydion's weak laugh died. "You're both too young and too old to get the reference.

Kirby didn't feel any amusement, but if she couldn't learn to smile in the face of destruction, the rest of her life was going to be miserable. "I know who Pinky and the Brain are." She and her immortals would figure out a solution, like they had this time. Maybe a little better than they had this time. "Where is everyone?"

Gwydion looked around her room. "I'm a little irritated Starkad kept you in this box for so long."

"It's a regular-sized bedroom." And a whole lot larger than what she'd had on campus. "You didn't answer my question."

"I told him there wasn't room in here. There's not. He'll want to know you're awake."

Kirby hesitated on her next question, but she had to know. "Min?" He wasn't here? "Brit?" Probably gone on her way. Maybe she took a little more of Starkad's money first. Or Min's.

"Checked into a nearby hotel. Brit left their room numbers. Min left an invitation to dinner."

Kirby smiled. Things to be grateful for. "I should tell Starkad I'm awake. If my doctor is going to let me out of bed."

Gwydion tipped her chin up with his finger and brushed his lips over hers. Heat and reassurance danced over her skin. "Reluctantly," he murmured against her lips. "But I have a hard time denying you anything you want. Now. Always. Forever."

"You're sappy and a dork. And I love you for it." Kirby kissed him back, but she felt the depth of his words. "I'm glad I'm back."

He rested his forehead against hers. Heat and comfort flowed between them, and she felt tension fade. "Me too. I'd really like to demand that you promise me…" He sighed.

"Not to do something like that ever again?" She wished she could.

"I know, it's who you are. So I'm going to focus on being grateful you're here now." Gwydion kissed her again, with an intensity that sank into her soul. "You should tell Starkad you're awake."

She nodded, tangled her fingers with Gwydion's, and hopped out of bed.

It was disorienting, walking through this house again. The opposite side of the coin from going back into TOM as Brit. Kirby's life had started here, as far as she was concerned. Knowing what she did now, she wouldn't take back any of it—not even the painfully celibate years of sexual tension with Starkad.

Who met her as soon as she turned the corner into the living room, pressing her to the wall with a growl and crushing his mouth to hers.

This was different than any other kiss they'd shared, and she couldn't put words to the *why*. She gripped the short hairs at the base of his neck and pressed her body into his, memorizing every sensation. Every emotion. Every sound and scent and taste.

Starkad pulled away and cupped her cheek while he studied her with a heated gaze. "I wanted to do that the first time I brought you here."

"I know." Six months ago, Kirby was still furious about the secrets he'd kept. She now understood so much more about everyone here than she ever would have asked to know.

"You only have the slightest idea." He slid his hand to the back of her head, to grip her hair and tug. "Because I'm going to fuck you in every place I've fantasized about doing so."

Desire flooded her body, carried on the wash of desires that lived in the shadows of this house. "Not all today."

"Maybe all today."

"It's too cold for nude sunbathing."

Starkad nipped her bottom lip. "We'll improvise."

Gwydion wrapped an arm around her waist. "Sounds like my kind of party."

Things weren't completely better, but this part of her life here, the bit that involved the three of them, was as close to perfect as they'd ever been.

Maybe it was selfish of her, to want to add two more people to the mix, but as much as she loved Starkad and Gwydion, there was still a pit inside that missed Min and Brit.

And Kirby wanted to heal those invisible wounds.

CHAPTER THIRTY-TWO

Kirby wasn't surprised that Min's version of *getting a hotel room nearby* was booking the top floor of the closest Four-Star hotel. An unfamiliar flavor of trepidation flowed through her as she knocked on his door.

He answered, looking very much the imposingly friendly god she'd fallen in love with so many times. He wore a look of surprise. "Kirby."

Huntress is fine. She swallowed the correction. They weren't there yet. She wanted to be, but their relationship had to evolve on its own. "I would have called, but…"

"You wanted to catch me off guard." Min's reply spoke to a new concern she had.

She'd seen him—not Erek, but Min—slide into the role of *soldier* with ease, on campus. It was what they needed at the time, but it had never been what she wanted. "I came to accept your dinner invitation. To tell you in person. And to talk someplace private."

"Come in." He opened the door wider. "Have a seat."

She hovered near the entrance instead. Things had to be said before she could get comfortable. "Are you staying in town for a while, or are you heading back home?" Not what she wanted to ask.

"*Home*'s been a rather transient concept for me for nearly three decades."

Since she was killed in L.A.

"Besides, I promised to make you fall in love with me again, and it's difficult to do that from across the country," Min said.

Her smile wavered at the reminder. There was no easy way to segue to this topic, and if she tried, she'd dance around the subject all night. "When I sent you away, I wanted you to understand me, not become me.

"And I wanted the same."

"I do understand you now." Thanks in part to living in Brit's thoughts. So many repressed emotions, and all of them potent in a way Kirby didn't dare feel. It was harder to hide them if she acknowledged them, but there was no reason to hide from her heart anymore. As welcome as the thought was, it also terrified her. "I understand the desire. The driving passion. The reason you searched for me, life after life. I get it."

Min's stance was casual, as he lounged against a nearby wall. It had taken her years to do something like that naturally, rather than falling into an at-ease posture.

"Being Erek didn't turn me into him, any more than being Brit turned you into her," Min said. "His knowledge sits in my head. His emotions and motivations as well. Similar to having read a well-written book. I'm not him, but I do understand your recent past much better, thanks to him."

"Okay. Good." Kirby had expected a more tension-filled conversation. "Then... um... I'd love to have dinner with you, and I'll see you then?" She'd never really done *dating* before. She and Brit had gone out to dinner a few times, but it was always part of a mission, because that was easier than sneaking into town and risking getting caught.

"You most certainly will. Before you go, will you do me a favor?"

Anything. It was easy to let the impulse in, and impossible to ignore it. "Depends on the favor."

Min tipped up her chin with a barely-there touch. "I've had lifetimes with you—not long ones, but many of them—and we have eternity ahead of us. I intend to claim your heart."

"I'm going to let you try." Kirby didn't understand the request. Hadn't they agreed that was where their relationship went next?

"But go visit Brit while you're here. Spend the afternoon with her. Being her won't have erased the hurt between you, but if it gave you the desire to try, now's the time to start."

Kirby had intended to talk to Brit. Maybe not today, but Min's request was a good nudge. "You're not going to lecture me on her intentions?"

He shook his head. "Those details are between you and her. I'd tell you she means it when she says she loved you, but you know that."

"I do." *Loved*, past tense. But the potential was there for something new to exist. Kirby was conflicted about wanting another chance, which didn't stop the feeling from being. "Thank you."

Min grasped her fingers and kissed the back of her knuckles. "I'll see you soon."

The warm glow Min left in Kirby's heart didn't diminish her apprehension. She wanted to have this conversation with Brit, but at the same time, she could stand to put it off a few more days. Not that her thoughts would be any more collected then than they were now.

She took the stairs down two flights, using the rhythm of her footsteps as a point for focus. What was she going to say?

I don't know.

What did she hope Brit would say?

As long as it's the truth, it doesn't matter.

Not completely true. Kirby hoped for some level of reconciliation, but she'd rather have honesty, than compliance.

Knocking on Brit's door was harder than Kirby expected. When Brit answered within seconds, she eliminated any remaining time for second-guessing.

"Hey." Brit looked surprised. She was wearing lightweight pajama bottoms and a camisole with nothing underneath.

Once upon a time, Kirby would have drooled all over herself at the casually sexy look. Who was she kidding? It was still fucking hot. There was just a lot more baggage to sift through, to enjoy the view.

"Can we talk?" Words that were supposed to be a death knell for relationships. Since she and Brit had both conquered death, a new beginning would be nice instead.

Brit stepped aside and swept her arm toward the room.

Kirby stepped inside. "Nice place. Living the high life, huh?" The lightness in her voice sounded as forced as it was.

"Min insisted. He's also given me access to all of his hotels, for as long as I want. He doesn't really do *understated*."

Not by default. "Never without an argument." Would that change now that he'd lived someone else's life? Unlikely, since he'd done so before. This wasn't the time to ponder Min. "Can I have the grand tour?" Kirby asked.

Brit raised an eyebrow. "This is the main room. Bedroom's back there. I have two TV's, can you imagine?" Her voice was flat.

"Two beds? Second one for eating takeout on?"

One corner of Brit's mouth tugged up. "And more space in that one bedroom than my entire apartment on campus."

The perfect segue. Kirby shoved aside hesitation. "Life sucked in that place. For both of us."

She expected Brit's infamous *I feel nothing* mask to slide into place. Instead, she clenched her jaw.

"I knew that. And yet when I got back, even seeing it through your eyes, I still found myself wondering why you left." It was a painful confession for Kirby to make, because it spoke more to her own fucked-up psychology than Brit's. "With Mark gone, they would have worshiped you."

"You're serious?"

"I'm honest. We haven't been kind to you. You've been talked down to, demeaned, and imprisoned. And Starkad is..." Justified but unkind.

"An asshole, yeah," Brit said bluntly. "But he's direct about it. Min's provided for me, despite not owing me anything. Gwydion treated me when I was injured. You let them."

Let. "It's not like they needed my permission."

Brit bit off a sharp laugh. "But if you'd told them not to, they would have complied. Regardless, how many Nobles do you think were actually my friends? How many of them *wouldn't* eliminate me the first chance they got?"

"Every single one of them would have." Ice Queen may have regretted it for a few seconds, but she still would have done it. "But they hadn't tried yet. I would have trusted them if I were you. I *did*, and I was." Until they tied a soldier to a tree, to kill him. Until they kicked down Loki's door. The last of Kirby's illusions about TOM were shattered in those short hours. It never should have taken her that long to catch on.

"That's how they knew you weren't me. You trusted them." Brit turned away and moved farther into the room. She paused next to the counter that divided kitchenette from living room, and flipped through a hotel notepad. "It's one of the reasons I loved you. I've never wondered where I stand when it comes to you. Whether it's love or disdain, you don't hide your feelings."

How was Kirby supposed to respond? Maybe the words were rhetorical.

Brit faced her again. "I'm sorry. For betraying you. For thinking you were anything like them. For every time I placed my comfort over your life. I didn't know how to deal with it, but I loved you then. I'm pretty sure I still do."

"I know." There was no need to wonder how much sincerity was in Brit's confession. Kirby had felt the reality of these words. She moved into the room as well, leaving the safety of the door behind. Not that she believed Brit would hurt her, but the instinct to give herself a rapid exit was still there.

"Side-effect of living in my head, I suppose," Brit said.

"But it doesn't overwrite what I lived or how I experienced it. I've seen how you feel, what you meant every time…" *you betrayed me.* "It still hurts, though I understand your side of things now. If I hadn't seen that your outlook has changed, it wouldn't matter what you intended. I wouldn't be here."

"That's fair. It doesn't mean I like it, but it's reasonable." Brit sighed heavily and sank into a nearby chair. "Since the very first day I met you, you've tried to protect me. Even when I was shot in the warehouse, you were there watching over me.

Just once, I'd like to be the one…" Another sigh, this one softer.

Something else Kirby never recognized until she saw the world from Brit's perspective. "You were the one, when it came to Hel. You did that"— *betrayed me*—"to keep me safe." Fucked up, but true.

"My point is I don't want you looking out for me forever."

Kirby had seen the sentiment, but it wasn't one that made sense to her, even now. "That's what partners do—look out for each other." Starkad had her back. Gwydion too.

Brit opened her mouth.

"I'm not talking about a one-way street. I never wanted to be your guardian, with you hiding behind me. I know you saw things that way, but I wanted us to be equals. You look out for me, and I look out for you. Until I was sharing your thoughts, I never realized how different your perspective on us was."

"And I never understood how you couldn't see the lack of balance."

"I didn't want to." It was easier for Kirby to be believe her intentions were all that mattered, regardless of how many ways Brit tried to say otherwise. "I'd do things differently this time."

"I'm sorry. Still. Again. Over and over, until I prove I mean it. Ever since I found out you were alive…"

Kirby leaned against the table, next to Brit. It was a complicated feeling, especially when she tried to put it into words.

"Do you think we could ever be *us* again?" Brit asked.

Kirby shook her head. "No."

"Oh." The single syllable carried so much hurt and disappointment.

"But I think we could be something better." Kirby hadn't been sure until she said the words aloud. "Something more equal, given a little bit of time." And a lot of healing. And talking. And more healing.

Brit stood, brushed her lips over Kirby's, and pulled back to search her face.

Kirby leaned in and returned the kiss. It might as well have been their first, for as different as it felt from the past. There was no more, *Oh my god, she likes me too.* Instead, there was a whole lot of, *Is this a mistake? It feels right. Can we actually work?*

The desire was there, lingering under years of hurt and aching to be recognized.

Brit stepped back. "Your guys aren't going to come after me for this, are they?" Hesitation undercut her teasing tone.

"No."

"It's weird, knowing that you know so much about me now. Could I do the same in return? Crawl inside your head and get a feel for you?" Brit asked.

"You don't want to be there." For a while, even Kirby didn't want to be in her own head. "Though in a way, you always have been."

"Gwydion said the same thing about you."

Kirby wasn't surprised. "He has a lot of the same scars I do. Then again, so do you and I." She leaned in, but hesitated for a heartbeat before claiming another kiss. Her heart ached as it slammed against her ribs. This wasn't the same kind of fear she felt the first time she met Gwydion and Min in this life, when she was throwing caution to the wind to escape her past.

This *was* her past, and with time, effort, and a lot of reestablished boundaries, it might be her future as well.

Brit's lips were soft and plump. Delicious and inviting. She glided her palms up Kirby's stomach, heat searing through fabric, and dragged her mouth down Kirby's jaw to kiss along her neck.

Kirby tugged her backward without looking, to fall onto the couch, and Brit landed to straddle one leg. Everything about this tied to their missions together. The physical was the same, but the emotion underneath ran deeper—a chasm of bittersweet, lined with cords of darkness and slivers of light.

Brit ground her weight into Kirby's thigh. Instinct drove now, whispering which buttons to push, and anticipating pleasure in return. Kirby teased Brit's breast, dragging a thumb over her nipple. They dove into hungrier kisses. Whimpers overlapped sighs. Desire flooded Kirby's veins.

"Wait." Brit's protest was weak, as she pulled away. She wavered as she stumbled to her feet. "I don't know if I want this to become sex. Or rather, I do. Desperately. But… not today."

"You're probably right. I guess I'll finish myself off when I get home." She shouldn't have let the teasing slip out, but it was too late to take the words back.

"You're allowed to do that?" Brit looked amused and sounded surprised. "Multiple gorgeous men at your beck and call, and you diddle yourself?"

Diddle. The phrasing almost made Kirby laugh. "I don't do it often, especially alone, but the intimacy in this room, it's between the two of us. It's not meant for sharing."

"I mean, if we're both going to masturbate anyway…" Brit stepped back to the wooden chair by the table, turned it, and sat, gaze never leaving Kirby. She caught her bottom lip between her teeth.

If they weren't touching each other, was it technically sex? How did this make Kirby feel more like a shy teenager again than anything about her current sex life? "I do like an audience."

"So I've seen."

The building shifted under Kirby, the motion escalating to a rolling shake that sent dust spilling into the air. It was worse than the quake they'd felt on the TOM campus.

Fear splashed over Brit's face. "This is what I felt when Loki killed the others. But bigger."

And it was close enough to threaten to bring a hotel down around them. *Fuck.*